In The Moment

A Novel

By: H.E. Burford

In The Moment: A Novel

This is a work of fiction; therefore, names, characters, references, places, events, experiences, and incidents are fictional or are a developed creation of the author's imagination and should be regarded as such.

ISBN #979-8-218-47606-9

Cover Image: Heather Burford

Printed in the United States of America

Contents

DEDICATION

To my husband who would lasso the moon for me if he thought it was in his reach.

To all the women who sit in anticipation waiting for something to happen. Make it happen for yourself. Start enjoying every *Moment.*

Introduction

Max was the love of my life: Tall, dark, handsome and very intelligent. Seems a little cliché, but to the naked eye, he was perfect. He had this charismatic way of making me think he was basically flawless and that even when I did nothing wrong, it was still my fault. I adapted over the years to his gas lighting; I even fully believed I was to blame. It ended poorly, but up until the very end, I was convinced I was in love with this man. In my eyes, he could do no wrong. I remained under his spell until I could no longer look blindly into his eyes or the reflection in the mirror.

What I never told anyone, including Max, is that when I left, I left because one of his sordid affairs resulted in the whore getting pregnant. He was unaware that I knew of his floundering about. Nothing came of the relationship, at least to my knowledge, as she apparently took off to the Midwest to raise their love child alongside her parents. I refused to have the dark cloud of his infidelity hanging over my head for eternity, so I decided it was time to leave.

I loved him madly, deeply, completely, and I couldn't allow myself to continue to feel this pain. I needed time to grieve the life I thought I deserved; to accept the reality of my situation. So, I gathered my feelings and my belongings and decided to move on with my life. Afterall, my misery wasn't owned by him, and neither was my joy. I was the only one who had control over these things. It just took me a long time to realize and accept it. To truly understand the heartache that was and still is, Max, I'd have to start at the beginning.

Chapter 1-Strange Encounters

It was a cold, dreary morning at a Jersey subway station and the rain had poured for what felt like weeks. I looked like a drowned rat and of course had left my apartment without so much as an umbrella. I was dressed in my nicest interview outfit; black dress pants that were a size too big, a white blouse with a hole in the sleeve, and an old black blazer I'd been wearing for special occasions such as this since early college. Of course, to top it off, I was wearing my lucky black heels which were now covered in rainwater and mud. I was hustling to grab the A train into New York for my first potential writing job as a columnist on a special interest piece. As I arrived at the station, I ran as quickly as my wet heels would let me to make the train in time for the 10 a.m. interview. As I approached the train, the doors began to close, and to my surprise, a tall gentleman threw his hands through the door to help keep it open long enough for me and my little black briefcase to get through. I smiled and slid past him, almost losing my briefcase; the case that included all of my portfolios and writing pieces that quite frankly I'd be willing to lose my arm over. The stranger grabbed my arm and safely helped me pull the briefcase on board. The train took off and I flounced toward the tall, handsome fella, into his arms.

"Thank you kind sir. I would have never made it without your help."
He grinned and nodded, saying nothing at all.
I shyly smiled back then looked down towards the ground as I held on to the pole in the center of the cart with my one free hand. He was holding on from the other side and I could feel him staring at me. Five stops passed and went without any words, and then the conductor called out my stop. As I looked

up and nodded, the gentleman let go of the pole and began to follow me out.

I hustled forward to exit, confused as to whether I hoped he'd approach me once again before parting ways or if I just preferred to make a run for it, avoid any embarrassment, and hopefully make it on time to my interview. I went with the latter and scurried up to the escalator. I glanced back and he appeared to still be following me. I headed out of the subway station and made a right towards the newspaper building. He was still right behind me, almost gaining on me at this point, and I began to feel overly anxious. My mind began to wander off, which was a frequent occurrence for me unfortunately. I had an awkward habit of overanalyzing everything. Was he interested in me or was he an ax murderer? Who knows? Admittedly, the chase felt exhilarating.

I turned and went through the revolving doors and then onto the elevator. As I approached the elevator attendant I said, "12th floor please." As I looked out of the elevator entrance I noticed him scurrying towards me, and at the last possible second he hopped on with me and said, "Good, you've already selected my floor."

Oh shit, I thought to myself, he's following me for sure. I continued to look forward and avoid eye contact. At this point I became increasingly uncomfortable. When we finally reached the 12th floor, we both stepped out as if we were together. I went to the reception counter as he sped past me and headed towards an office. I felt a little calmer with the realization that he at least appeared to work here and wasn't following me without purpose.

Disoriented still, I approached the receptionist.

"Hello, my name is Alicia. I'm here for a 10a.m. interview with Max Edwards. "

She smiled and responded, "Okay. Thank you. He'll be right out for you. Just take a seat."

I was unbelievably nervous, and I wished I had enough time to freshen up a bit, but I guess it's take me or leave me at this point. It was something short of a miracle that I even made it here at all, much less with time to spare. I sat there for what felt like forever, but realistically it was only about 20 minutes, when out came the tall, handsome stranger from an office. He continued towards me, and I was literally beside myself. As he approached I stood up and smiled.

" Well, we meet again. Hello, my name is Alicia. Alicia Lavy. Nice to formally meet you."

He stuck his hand out and shook mine gently, not firm like you'd expect from a man of his size and stature.

"I'm Max Edward's, Copy Editor for the paper and hiring manager for our special interest columns. Please, follow me."

Lord this wasn't good. How would I stay focused for an interview staring into those blue eyes? I kept mentally giving myself a pep talk, but it felt very ineffective. I was hooked. Job or no job, I fully planned on getting to know Mr. Max Edwards on a more personal level. Intrusive thoughts enveloped my mind, and I was just silently praying I could keep it together.

He started the interview nonchalantly, acting as if the events of the morning had never taken place. For some reason it was comforting; it helped me to stay focused, moderately blocking the racy thoughts that were eroding my mind.

He wasted no time in getting started.

"So, Mrs. Lavy, share with me some of your background and why you have an interest in writing for our column."

I giggled, which I was acutely aware was unprofessional as I blurted out, "Miss Lavy. It's Miss, not Mrs., I'm not married. Not yet anyway."

I couldn't just shut up. I had to add more than the obvious, but thankfully Mr. Edwards shrugged it off with a smile.

"Well excuse me, then, Miss Lavy. Same question regardless of your marital status." He snickered as well, which once again put me at ease.

"Well, I have been writing for years, primarily independent pieces, self-published of course, and I have a degree in journalism with an emphasis on mass communications. My original intent was to be on television. You know, like Barbara Walters, but I decided after some of my clinical courses in college that writing behind the screen was a little more my style. I have wanted to have my own column for as long as I can remember and I am very intrigued by and knowledgeable of the fashion and night life here in New York, so I thought this column would be a good fit."

He nodded. "Very interesting. Could I see one of your portfolios?"

"Certainly." As I handed one over to him, he began perusing the articles and nodding and smiling as in acceptance. I felt confident for a change. My nerves calmed down and I prepared myself to answer whatever questions he might throw at me. After several minutes of review, he looked up, smiled, and said, "It seems you have the style we are looking for. Let me share this with my boss and I will give you a call back within two days with our decision. Sound good?"

I stood up and reached my hand out to shake his and nodded in agreement. "I look forward to hearing from you Mr. Edwards."

"Most definitely, Miss Lavy, with an emphasis on "Miss," and just call me Max."

Here I go with the schoolgirl giggles again...

"Max. Thank you. I'll speak with you soon."

I gathered my things and headed towards the elevator. I felt like I should dance or scream or do something enthusiastic, yet I was still a little embarrassed by my alter ego, the bashful schoolgirl. I was as excited about the potential job opportunity as I was about getting to know Max better. For such a crappy start to the day, it sure was shaping up to be a good one.

The next two days were a whirlwind of emotions. I could not sit still to save my life. I was hoping Max would call soon after the interview and say that his boss was so excited to have me as part of their team that they couldn't wait two days to reach out. But now as the end of the second day was nearing, I became worried. Maybe he was still interviewing up until the last minute. Or maybe he was just busy and lost track of time. Regardless, I couldn't do anything but sit on the couch and stare at the television. I hadn't even had a real meal in two days. A couple of snickerdoodle cookies and a banana was pretty much all I had consumed since the interview. Of course, I had a few almonds and several cups of coffee, maybe a couple of string cheeses, but nothing substantial that would constitute a meal. I did have a few bottles of red wine; that was always a daily staple.

As four o'clock rolled around I decided maybe going to get something to eat would fill in the time gap from four to five and the food would most definitely do me some good. So, I grabbed my purse and headed down the street with my ringer on the highest decibel, to the closest deli and Bodega. I had just finished ordering my chicken salad sandwich on rye when my phone rang loudly. It startled me, and it really shouldn't have, as obviously I had been expecting the call. I smiled at Paul, the owner, and grabbed a seat. I placed my stuff on the table and answered in what I believed was my most professional and patient voice.

"Hello, this is Alicia Lavy."

"Hi, Alicia. Max Edwards here. I hope I am catching you at a good time."

"Most definitely, Mr. Edwards. I was just getting ready to grab a bite to eat."

"That's perfect. Where are you at if you don't mind me asking? I am famished and we could discuss your new position over a meal."

"New position? So, I am hired?" I was almost shrieking, and I tried my darndest to reel it in.

"Oh yes. I guess I should have led with that. So, dinner?"

"Well actually I'm just at a deli close to my apartment. I ordered a sandwich, nothing exciting. I could meet you somewhere else that has something a little more substantial to eat if you'd like."

"Perfect. It's 4:45 now. How about 6:30 at *Jolly's Grille* on Main?"

"I think I can do that. It's about a 30-minute taxi ride though and I need to run home real quick. Would 7 be okay? Maybe you could grab a snack to tide you over?"

"Sounds great, Alicia. I hope you're okay with me calling you Alicia."

"Definitely, Max," I giggled. "I'll see you at 7. Bye for now."

Max spoke as if he was nodding and smiling, I could just tell.

Max repeated back, "Bye for now."

In my head all I could think of was Lord, I've got to get some control over myself, and I grabbed my sandwich from the table, took a big bite and dumped the rest in the trash can on my way out. Paul smiled and nodded as I whispered "sorry." I knew we wouldn't appreciate me wasting his masterpiece of a sandwich.

I had to hurry home and change into something that would be both professional and attention grabbing. I was nervous, but honestly, it didn't really matter what the intended context of the evening was; it was all good news to me. I was excited to have an opportunity to get to know Max better, even if it was strictly professional. I was fully prepared to enjoy and live in this moment, regardless of the direction the dinner date took. More importantly. I wanted to remember this feeling and use it on days when things weren't as bright and cheery, a strategy my therapist shared with me that had been working well since I lost my father. This was going to be one of those moments, I could just tell, and I wanted to savor it. Hell, it already was. I was offered the job, and I get to have dinner with a gorgeous man. It doesn't really matter how the night ends. It's already a perfect moment to remember.

I basically sprinted back to my apartment and threw off the gym shorts and tank I was wearing and just dropped them on the floor. I ran to my closet and grabbed my black striped, sleeveless dress. It had a small slit on the left side that showed the proper amount of leg, and it cut just enough to acknowledge my cleavage without looking as if I was making the wrong statement or trying too hard. Desperate wasn't a good look for any woman, especially in the presence of a man like Max. I threw on my strappy black sandals and my dangly silver earrings and grabbed my purse as I ran out the door. It was 5:40 already and still at the tail end of rush hour, so my 30-minute ride could easily turn in to 60. I threw my hand in the air to hail a taxi. After four passed me by, a fifth taxi pulled up and stopped for me. I smiled and thanked him and then quietly said,

"Jolly's Grill on Main Street please."

I arrived at 6:30, 30 minutes before our date or meeting or whatever it was. I was happy that I was early because I knew it would give me a chance to get at least one drink in me to calm my nerves before Max arrived. I paid the cab driver and hustled into the restaurant. The bar was located close to the entrance and as I approached the only open bar stool, a man spun around and smiled. "Well, I guess you made it a bit early too."

Shit! He's already here. Keep it together.

A little irritated that I didn't have an opportunity to have a drink or two before meeting up, I still managed to keep my disappointment at bay and force a smile.

"Well, yes I did. Nice to see you again Max."

"What will it be, MISS Lavy? Emphasis on the Miss, of course."

I giggled inappropriately again. "Red. A glass of sweet red wine please."

"Okay. Super. Bartender. Can we have a glass of your finest sweet red wine please for this young lady?"

"Certainly, Max. But call me by my name next time. As often as you're in here I think we should be on a first name basis. Don't you?"

Max laughed and so did the bartender, James. I just sat there smiling like an idiot. I really needed a glass in me before we met up. Based on the familiarity with the bartender though, I had doubts that he would judge me too much if I had several glasses.

James sat the glass of wine down in front of me. I looked up at Max and said, "Forgive me for this." Then I grabbed the glass of red and downed it. "Another one please, James."

James and Max both smiled. James looked at me and said, "Certainly looks like you've met your match, Max."

He brought the second glass and I just sipped. I didn't want him to think I was a lush, but my nerves were shot. I was excited and scared at the same time and I just couldn't seem to get control over my emotions. After a few more sips, Max leaned in and said, "Should we go ahead and get a table?"

"Sure. If you're ready."

He stood up and grabbed his beer mug and my wine glass and headed towards the hostess. I felt a small sense of relief as I was really struggling to find the words to strike up interesting conversation. He was just so damn handsome and my desire to keep this new gig was heavily competing with that of ripping his clothes off. Max reached the hostess stand and smiled at her with that "do whatever I say" smile.

"Hello. We have a reservation for two at 7:00 for Edwards."

"Super. Right this way."

As I walked behind him I became increasingly uncomfortable with the fact that he had a reservation for us at a busy restaurant at such short notice. I wondered if he had already tentatively made a reservation and deliberately waited until the last minute to call me to force my hand at dinner tonight. Of course it would not have taken much persuasion. Or was it just that he was that well-respected and popular at this restaurant? Either way, the entire situation had me secretly begging to question his motives.

The hostess took us to a quaint table for two, right by the front window.

You could see the night life unfolding across the river in NYC from our seats; it was a fantastic spot for a dinner date, but very distracting for someone with ADHD, especially when in the company of someone who knew very little about me. I began to worry about keeping focus, so I decided to get the conversation started myself, and I was determined to keep it going. I wouldn't survive the evening if I became hyper focused on what was happening outside the window or even worse, if an awkward silence took over.

"So Max, is it customary to take new hires to elegant dinners overlooking the city?"

He smiled.

"No. This is a first."

I could tell by his reaction and mannerisms that he was interested in me, but I wanted to play it cool.

Still, I could feel myself blushing.

"So why then? What makes this situation different?"

"Well, it is unprofessional for certain, but your position is not under my direct supervision, at least not yet, so I figured we could make an exception."

I smiled coyly, but I knew deep down this was a bad idea. I really wanted to excel in this new position and my focus was already turned towards six feet of a beef cake. I continued to sip my wine and smile as Max spoke of random tidbits of information. After ten minutes or so of idle chit chat, I jumped in, headfirst, into the conversation.

"Max, hope you don't mind if I chime in, but I feel like maybe this meeting was more than just a little pre-meditated. What is your goal here? I'm not much of one for playing games. I mean, I'm single and not opposed to dating, but I am also very interested in being successful in this new job. Obviously, the job is my priority. So, what gives? Honestly."

"Well, well, well. Straight to the point. I like it. I am certainly not used to this straightforward approach in my experiences with women, and I have rarely heard a woman say that she prioritizes her career over a man. Don't take that the wrong way. I admire it and your honesty, but to be honest, I'm not even sure where to start."

Smiling still, to the point that my face was starting to ache a little, "Just start! I'll feel more at ease once I understand what you're hoping to gain from all of this."

Chapter 2- <u>Max</u>imum Opportunities

I listened intently as Max spoke, slowly nibbling on dessert and sipping what had to be my sixth glass of red. I had posed the question, that's true, but I certainly wasn't expecting all of this. He shared tidbits of his past relationships, his emancipation from his parents at the age of 15, and his start in the world of editing and publishing at the young age of 22. He spewed information at me like he had known me for years rather than hours, and I wasn't certain if I found it desirable or overwhelming for a first meeting or date or whatever this was. With all the sordid details he was sharing, he still hadn't addressed the purpose of meeting with me, not in a professional or personal capacity. With the last bite of Crème Brulé and the final swig of wine, I nudged back into the conversation.

"Max, sorry to interrupt. I truly appreciate you sharing so much of your experiences with me, but you seem to be skating around the real question. Is this purely professional? It doesn't feel like it, but as I mentioned with some emphasis at the beginning of this date, I am a planner. Big on communication. I need to know what I'm jumping in to."

"Well Alicia, I am in unchartered territory. As I have shared already, my previous relationships have been less than desirable. I have a demanding job. I work long hours and always have some deadline to meet, and unfortunately, most women just don't get it, so eventually they get fed up with my inconsistencies and split. When I met you this morning, I was immediately intrigued. Not at the office, but on the train. I noticed a lot of things about you, but the trendles of brown hair falling off the side of your face, damp from the rain shower, caught my attention first. Most women would have appeared disheveled, but you looked quite lovely, honestly. Most of your makeup had been washed off by the rain as well, but you remained unscathed. Your natural beauty cannot be denied. I'm not sure why you wear makeup at all as beautiful as you are without it. I got an immediate sense that you were the type of person who was almost always ready to roll with the punches. I didn't know you were my first interview, but I could tell you were traveling with intent. You had your briefcase which you absolutely refused to let go of, almost to the extent of losing your arm," Max said almost snickering. "I could tell by the way you were dressed that you were heading for something important to you and so often nowadays, people just arrive for interviews and business meetings wearing whatever they want, without any consideration for time and place. I had a woman show up in ripped up jeans and a dirty t-shirt last week. I didn't even waste time interviewing her. I just told her the position was filled. So, I was attracted to your presentation, your effort, and your clear focus, but honestly, your beauty caught my attention first. And then when I formally met you at the interview I just couldn't shake the idea that this was fate. I wanted to ask you out on the train, but I too was running late for an interview. Obviously, yours. I couldn't just let this opportunity slip through my fingertips. I believe most things happen for a reason. So, I thought, What the hell? The icing on the cake for me was that your professional goals and understanding of this line of work were evident from the moment you began speaking and luckily, they were aligned with mine. I totally understand if you are uncomfortable with all of this, and I can remain professional if need be. Afterall, you are obviously overqualified for this position, so we are overjoyed to have you write for us, but if you are feeling any of the things I am, I'd like to see where this can go between us too."

I just knew I looked crazy staring back at him with my mouth hanging open. I was shocked to say the least, and I couldn't come up with words. Any words. And this was a rare occurrence for me. I just sat there and stared at him. Eventually, I managed to smile and utter, "aha. Yes. Yes I am interested. In both. The job and seeing where this could go."

That's all I could muster up. Luckily he nodded and smiled again and then flagged the waiter down for our check. After he settled the bill, he walked to my side of the table and pulled my chair out and in true gentleman fashion, helped me to my feet. As we were leaving the restaurant, I felt like I was floating, and I really wished I could get some control over myself. I knew that I should play a little harder to get, but I just couldn't resist this man. I was smitten. He seemed so perfect in every possible way.

Max flagged down a taxi and said, "Just one stop please," and I knew that this was most likely going to end badly, but I just didn't care. I had never went home with a man after a first date. Hell, I hadn't even after five dates. I always waited until I knew the relationship was solid and exclusive. I couldn't take my eyes off him though and I just didn't care about right or wrong. All I knew was that I wanted him, and he wanted me, and that's all I needed to know at this moment.

Chapter 3- Jersey and The Whore

Max and I dated for about three months before we tied the knot. We had one of those cliché destination weddings in the Bahamas, and because neither of us had any family to speak of, it was just the two of us. It was magical, I must admit. The entire week was like a fairytale, but once we returned to the city, things immediately began to change.

I had a pregnancy scare right after the honeymoon. It was more than a scare. I was in fact pregnant. Three months in, to be exact, when I miscarried. I was devastated, but Max seemed relieved. Looking back, his relief is what destroyed me. He had no empathy for me, and he did not grieve at all, at least not in my presence. I decided then and there that the two of us would never have children together, and soon after I went to my doctor and asked to have my tubes tied. Because I was married and without children, Max had to sign off on the procedure, which he did almost with enthusiasm. In retrospect, I should have left then, but Max had a way about him. He was so charismatic that I made excuses for him to myself. All he had to do was give me that coy smile and a fake apology, then wrap me in his arms, and I was over the heartache for the night.

As days became years, Max made excuses to stay in the city for business meetings. I knew the ins and outs of the job too well to believe his bullshit, but I looked the other way because I wanted him to come back to me after he was finished with his "business."

Max and I had a quaint home in a suburb in Jersey. It was close to the A train and made commutes to New York city easy. I was happy there, which helped me for a while to disregard Max's philandering and deceitful behavior. I could do most of my writing from home and Max had built me a beautiful sitting area in the backyard with flowers and twinkling lights. It was the perfect spot for me to watch the sunset, to have a glass of wine, and to write without disruption. But a house isn't a home without someone to love in it. Or at least that was what I had been taught growing up, so I always felt the emptiness on a deeper level in Max's absence. He may have loved me still, but I struggled pretending that he hadn't just kissed and touched someone else hours before returning to me. I was still so in love with Max, and I was so attracted and attached to him, that I allowed him to throw his arms around me and be with me whenever he was willing; I pretended that everything was fine each time he returned so the attention would continue. I yearned for his attention and his touch, so I did my best to overlook the rest. And when he was home, we acted like we were in love. Sadly, it wasn't an act for me, and that pain was suffocating.

Our neighborhood used to be a dangerous area until the city initiated regentrification projects and so though the housing was quite lovely, the original stores remained untouched. They were in need of revamping, but I liked that about our neighborhood. I appreciated the authenticity of it. I knew all the owners of the shops and restaurants within walking distance, and they knew me. With everything else always feeling uncertain, I found comfort in this detail.

So, I made it work for me. The infidelity. The spontaneous late-night meetings. The fake love making. All of it. It wasn't until year fourteen that I ran head on into Dominque Jefferson at the local bodega. I wouldn't have paid her any attention except for the necklace she was wearing. It stood out, and for good reason, it was mine. A one of a kind that Max had given me for our second wedding anniversary, and I stood there in the bodega, flabbergasted. Was it mine? Did Max have another made? When was the last time I saw my necklace? I just couldn't let it go, so I walked over to the tall, red-haired beauty, who would have stood out in this neighborhood regardless of the necklace, but even more so with my emerald and diamond pendant on.

"Excuse me. I couldn't help but notice that beautiful necklace you are wearing. It's quite unique. Wherever did you find it?

She looked at me and smiled, in a way that made me unnerved. I was prepared for just about any response as she opened her perfectly lined and glossed lips.

"Well honey, it's a hell of a story, but I'll give you the Cliff's Notes version. I was driving through the upper west side when I felt a thump and boom. Of course, as luck would have it, I blew a tire. I rarely go into the city because you know, parking is a bitch, but I needed to have a document signed at my lawyer's office, so I thought what the hell, I'll do a little shopping while I'm already in town. I had just pulled into the parking lot when the tire gave out and of course, I'm not a change my own tire type of gal. I mean look at these perfectly manicured nails. I wasn't about to mess them up for a tire, so I flagged down the first nice looking gentleman I saw. By the looks of him, I was guessing he hadn't changed too many tires in his lifetime either, but desperate times you know. Anyway, long story short, he changed my tire and my life. Sounds cliché right? But it's exactly how it happened. It was love at first sight. I'm sure you didn't need all the details, but Max, that's my beau's name, gave this to me on our three-month anniversary, which was the point of me dragging on with all these details of our love story. That's how I ended up with this beauty. It's one of a kind, just like my Max. You'll have to forgive me, doll. I just love to talk. I have never met a stranger. Good thing too or I wouldn't have met this wonderful man. I never did ask where he found it, but I do remember him saying it was specifically made for me. So sadly, you couldn't get one for yourself if you wanted to. But when I see Max, I'll ask for the name of the jeweler. Give me your card and I'll text you with the details."

I stood there with my mouth hanging open. I prayed she couldn't tell how distraught I was. I pulled myself together to form words.

"Well, it is lovely. And that's a great story. Max, you say. Do you two live around here?"

I knew I had seen my necklace in the last few months. I remembered wearing it to the 9th wedding anniversary dinner. And apparently she had been special enough to receive the same quality gift after just three short months. It took me several years, but whatever. This was some bullshit and I needed to remain collected for the rest of this damning conversation.

"We don't live together so I thought since I was in the neighborhood I'd grab him his favorite sandwich from this bodega. He's always raving about it. And then call him and surprise him. I'm thinking maybe a picnic in the park. Do you know of any parks close by?

Where are my manners? My name is Dominque Jefferson. And your name is?"

"Um, Sally. Sally Johnson. And yes, there are several parks close by, but I'd ask your boyfriend, Max, is it? I'm sure he will know of the perfect place."

I felt a force inside me, encouraging me to repeat his name to her as many times as I could, in hopes that she would correct me and say Mark or Mike. But no, it was Max. That bastard!

I'm not even certain where I came up with my pseudo name. I'm just glad I did instead of blurting out Alicia, wife of your adulterous boyfriend.

"I don't have any cards on me, but if you give me yours, I'll reach out to you. Maybe we can even meet for lunch sometime when you're on this side of town."

"Sounds perfect, doll. I'm going to grab that sandwich now. Pleasure to have met your acquaintance."

"Likewise. Enjoy your picnic," I said almost too convincingly.

She grinned and spun back towards the counter.

I headed towards the exit without any consideration at all for what I was doing there in the first place.

Once I knew of the affair, which appeared to be an actual serious relationship rather than just another whore for the evening, I decided enough was enough. I didn't leave him immediately. I took the time to befriend Dominque. I got close enough to have all the proof I might need in a divorce settlement. Before I could finalize our divorce, I had lunch one last time with Dominque. I explained to her that I had found an opportunity elsewhere and would be moving soon. She had nonchalantly shared that her boyfriend had a wife and that he was planning on leaving her. I could hardly believe the words coming out of her mouth. We had met for lunch enough times now that I was starting to really like her. I had thought several times to myself that if she knew the truth and dumped Max, we might become real friends. The guilt I had been feeling was trumping my hatred for what Max was doing to me, and as I pondered telling her the truth, she shared another huge secret with me. With enthusiasm, she blurted out that she was pregnant.

I jumped to my feet and immediately revealed my real identity. I then proceeded to fill her in on what a lying, conniving, piece of shit Max really was. I encouraged her to stay with him, as it was evident they deserved each other. Any woman who would willingly mess around with another woman's husband was pure trash in my book.

As I grabbed my purse and headed to the exit I looked back at her one last time and said,

"Dominque, karma is a real bitch. When you were dreaming and praying for the perfect man, you should have known that God would never answer your prayers with another woman's husband. Think about that when you and your child are sitting at home alone while Max is off galivanting with another woman."

I was packed and gone in days, and from what I understood, she decided to leave Max too. I never discussed it with Max, though I'm certain she gave him an earful. Our paperwork was all but signed and finalized, so I just left a note and the packet with signatures, and never looked back.

Our marriage was as much of a whirlwind as our courtship, and though I managed to stretch it out for a little over 9 years, Max was never fully satisfied with commitment. It wasn't just me. He just wasn't a one-woman man. I think that's why he felt relief when I lost our baby. Too much commitment. Too much expectation. He wasn't satisfied with just one of anything, not even in his career. He bounced from publishing company to news outlet, making career changes as frequent as some change their underwear.

I knew this about him, and I still let him pursue me.

I accept some of the blame, but moving on and

finally letting go, that was entirely up to me. And I

was more than ready.

Chapter 4: New York/New Beginnings

After leaving Max and the life I had known for the

past nine years, I decided that maybe getting an

apartment in the city would be a good fit for me. I

was lucky enough to find a rent-controlled apartment

near the editing office for my column, and I lived

close enough to most of the hot spots in New York

to at least witness some of the night life to

authenticate my writing. I rarely went out though,

and I never made any close friends aside from Janice

and Bob who both had worked on editing my

column since I began working there. Janice wasn't

really a social butterfly and Bob was married and

rarely went out unless his wife could find childcare. It

was important to him that she could go as well. I

respected Bob for putting his wife first, something I

was quite unfamiliar with, so I rarely invited him

anywhere as I didn't want to cause any undue stress in his marriage.

For most of my time in the big city, I stayed huddled up in my tiny apartment, ordering Chinese takeout most nights, and sipping red wine on the fire escape. It was lonely and loud and not at all peaceful like my Jersey patio. The only twinkling lights I saw on a regular basis were those from the water tower in the distance and the trash trucks that made their rounds at 4:45 a.m. and 6:30 a.m. respectively. The fragrance of sweet-smelling flowers was replaced with the smell of sewage, and every once and a while, the scent of urine from a drunk passerby, usually a tourist who couldn't handle their liquor or the nightlife that NYC had to offer.

My early memories of spending time in New York were more pleasant. Before marrying Max, I frequented the clubs regularly. Given that I was much younger then, I loved the busyness of the city. I enjoyed walking to the A train and reading the *Times* on my way to an internship or class. I loved the smell of coffee from a local bodega, and I didn't take notice of the smell of trash or urine, or the obnoxious way tourists trashed the city when they visited. My perspective had changed drastically over the years, and I yearned for quiet now, for peace and tranquility. Even when I first met Max that morning so many years ago on the train in the pouring rain, all in a hustle to get from one point to the next, I felt exhilarated, and I appreciated the city for all it afforded me and my budding career. Now it was just another reminder of how my life was stale, never changing, and exhaustively lonely.

I made it 13 years in New York city alone, but on my 44th birthday, I decided that I'd had enough of the city. I needed to find happiness. I wanted to feel the salty breeze of the ocean hit my face. And more than anything else, I wanted to find a few friends and someone or something else to love. I arranged to continue writing for my column remotely, as I was doing that all but two days a week already. I looked online for a place that seemed peaceful and endearing and came upon a small coastal town in Maine. As I sat there staring at the computer screen, I wondered if this could be the answer I had been looking for. Sure, I might be alone for a while as I adjust to my new surroundings, but instead of garbage trucks and the scent of decay, I could smell the fresh air rolling in, gently kissed with a sprinkle of salt, and maybe fresh baked pastries from the local coffee shop, *The Beanery,* which was advertised on the town's tourism page. I could look out on the horizon and see the 150-year-old lighthouse and watch the sunset on the boardwalk. I was sold!

It all seemed too good to be true, but I was willing to risk it for a chance to feel peace within; something I had been lacking for myself since just after I married Max. So, I sublet my New York City apartment, packed my things, and headed to Fary Banks, Maine, and never looked back.

Chapter 5-Breaking the Cycle- Maine

I showed up at *The Beanery* at 9:30 a.m. like I had every Tuesday morning since I moved here. For the first five years or so, I went for coffee with no agenda. I would come and start my column pieces or simply just people watch. This week I felt different. I was tired of being alone and I decided it was time to make a move. I thought to myself, what's the worst that could happen? Someone would snarl at me and walk away? Hell, they'd been doing that indirectly for six years anyway. So, I sat there, with my latte, scanning the room for any opportunity to make a friend. I was deep in the trenches of my own gut; trying desperately to find something or someone to fill the void that years of heartache and loneliness had left me with. The beach and the salty air and the beauty that enveloped Fary Banks helped, but it didn't completely fill the emptiness inside. And as luck would have it, I had no success today. No one seemed approachable or they looked as if they were in a big hurry, and I didn't want to bother them. I continued to make excuses.

Several more Tuesdays cycled, and I wondered again, what was wrong with me? I never really tried to make friends in New York; I had just accepted that loneliness was part of the gig, but I had such high hopes for this small town. In small towns, people are supposed to be welcoming, but my experience had been quite the opposite. I had even been referred to as a "come here" on many occasions; opposed to the "from heres" who were born and raised in Fary Banks. I had all but given up when I noticed a rather attractive, middle-aged man walking in. He was tall, about 6 foot if I were to guess, with broad shoulders, and man was he easy on the eyes. I heard the barista refer to him as Jeff as he approached the counter to grab a pickup order. His most dominant feature was without a doubt, his piercing, cat-like eyes. They were a shiny green, with an almost sparkling glare that captivated me upon entry. The sun was beating down through the glass doors and struck the top of his salt and pepper hair and met up directly with those eyes. He noticed me almost immediately, and shyly, I looked down at my phone on my lap to avoid direct eye contact, hoping he didn't realize I had been sizing him up for the past few minutes. Once I looked back up to see if he had left, Jeff grinned at me through his peppered mustache and gave me a little wink with his left eye. I'm guessing he winks out of habit when he smiles. I do that too. His beard had been trimmed recently and I thought it to be unbelievably sexy. In the past few years, I had found myself increasingly more attracted to mature gentlemen; men with a little more shape and well-groomed facial hair with a little pepper sprinkled throughout. Men become more distinguished, and let's face it, seem to improve with age. Unfair, I thought to myself. Women seem to age like milk, and here this 50 something year old man is aging like fine wine. I continued to stare at Jeff, scanning in all his features without trying to look too obvious or desperate, and I quickly took notice that a ring wasn't present on the wrong finger. Suddenly, I wished I had fixed myself up a tad more, though he didn't seem to mind as he hadn't taken his eyes off of me since he entered the coffee house, aside from requesting the order. He grabbed his to go order and walked by my corner table nudging the chair with his cell phone, which was oddly attached to the side of his hip. Very old school, but I liked it. He smiled and then said in a deep, almost husky voice, "Hello there Darlin."

My tongue-tied dumb ass couldn't speak. I knew he was speaking to me, but I was struggling to believe it. I mustered up the confidence to say "Hello" back and oddly enough, he continued speaking to me. "I'm in a rush right now, but I couldn't help but notice you sitting here all alone. Odd to me. Someone pretty like you should be sharing your time with someone...maybe even me?"

He half snickered as the craziness came out of his mouth. What a line, I thought to myself, but I was intrigued. At this point I had not responded with anything more than a nod and a giggle, and of course that shallow, "Hello." He made me feel so nervous for some reason. It had been a while since I had been pursued by a man, and I still felt a little gun shy after Max. I knew it had been close to 20 years since Max and I ended, but the pain was always fresh in my mind, and that had prevented me from pursuing any other serious romantic relationships. As I became lost in my own head, per usual, I thought to myself, speak idiot. He's going to think you're mute and leave.

He continued the charade with minimal participation from me, of course. "How about coffee Thursday morning, around the same time?"

My intrigue turned to awe. Kind of presumptuous of him. He didn't even know if I was available. Do I look that lonely? Does it seem that impossible to this man that I might have a fella already? These thoughts, these negative thoughts, overtook my mind and prevented me from responding like a normal person. Never able to take a compliment, I looked down from his shiny hazel gaze and muttered, "Sure...I am free Thursday morning."

Jeff smiled again. "Cool beans...I'll see you then Darlin. Enjoy your day."

I nodded in acceptance and smiled shyly again, then looked back down at my half empty latte. Cool beans? Who the hell says, "cool beans?" As he was leaving *The Beanery* I decided that "cool beans" was a much better response than nodding and complete silence, which apparently, is all I am capable of.

And it was at that point that I decided I was going give this date everything I had in me, even if it was just for coffee. I was lonely, and this was an opportunity with a handsome man who seems to be interested in me. This date was going to be perfect if I had anything to do with it. I wasn't going to be my regular, negative self. I had to get out of my own head and believe I could be happy again. Maybe this wasn't the "one" per say, but it was a shot at meeting someone new, and maybe all the sorrow from my past wouldn't continue to drown me if I replaced a little of it with something cheerful.

Thursday. Maybe that will be the day that things start looking up for me.

Chapter 6-Not Quite Thursday

That evening, I searched my closet for the perfect outfit for my coffee date; I obviously didn't want to dress up too much, I mean it is only coffee, but I wanted him to see a better side of me than he encountered on Tuesday. Since he was already impressed with meager effort, I was sure to blow him away...or at least that was the plan. I simply wanted friendship, but if something more could develop, I was open to it. I had been alone more of my life than with someone, and the quality of those I had been with made me feel more alone in their presence than when I was all by myself. The thought of just the date itself caused a stir of flutters in my stomach; not sure if I'd call them butterflies, but it was a feeling I hadn't felt in a very long time, and it was nice.

I continued to scan my closet. Per usual, I had absolutely NOTHING to wear. The task would prove easier if I had not simply thrown all my clothes on the floor after trying them on. Piles of clothing, some too small and some too big began to pile up. Maybe if I had thrown away the pile of "maybe next year" or "maybe after I lose 10lbs" it would be easier to sift through the mess and find something appropriate. Just like the quest to find a friend or companion, the pursuit to permanently lose the same 10lbs that I kept losing and gaining had proven unsuccessful. I wanted to make a change. Many changes in fact. It's all about mindset. That's probably the most important lesson my therapist in New Jersey had taught me. I hadn't found a good therapist here in Fary Banks, but that was on my to do list. I needed to declutter everything: My mind, my closet, and by extension, my life. So, I went to the kitchen and grabbed some large trash bags.

I decided to create piles and bag up the too small items and drop them off somewhere this evening. Then I could justify doing a little shopping. Just a blouse or a nice accessory would make me feel better about this upcoming date with Jeff. And so, I gathered up the pile on the left side of the bed and placed it in the first bag. And I continued through my room and closet. And all at once, I felt relief. Less baggage already. Off to *The Plaza*, the local outdoor shopping mall, to find something new to wear. It will come together. I just know it!

Shopping in Fary Banks was scarce, so most took the ferry to neighboring towns. Other than mom and pop businesses, there weren't many options. So, it was off to Woodland to get the extras that Fary Banks couldn't provide. And the best place to do that in Woodland was *The Plaza*.

Once at *The Plaza*, one cab and a ferry ride away, I entered the closest clothing store and began to scan the place. It was always overwhelming for me to go shopping so I often avoided it and just ordered what I needed online. I have ADHD and the attention piece is quite overwhelming at times. I have the ability, thankfully, to fully scan a store and mentally highlight which direction to take for the speediest and most effective shopping experience. I noticed some colorful short sleeve blouses to the left of the store. I moved in that direction and scanned through the four racks that had size medium blouses on them. I also saw a few dresses; not too revealing, but still kind of sexy, and so I grabbed two of them as well. I then hustled to the dressing room to try on the items I had found, though I typically avoid dressing rooms at all costs. I hate them. And if it wasn't over an hour trip back to return the purchases, I would buy all the items and return what didn't fit later, but since these shopping trips were infrequent, maybe twice a month, I chose to make the sacrifice. As expected, the first top was way too snug. As I tugged at the right sleeve, my watch became stuck, and the neck of the blouse almost strangled me in the process. As I stood there, tangled in front of the mirror I thought to myself, this is it, Alicia. This is how it ends. Death by strangulation in a dressing room. I'm certain every woman has had this experience and it's almost as frightening as being stuck in a public bathroom without any toilet paper: No one around to help and stuck. After finally managing to escape the blouse, I found the other two to be adequate and one of the dresses to fit my curves appropriately; just a little bit of cleavage and folds in the linen that seemed to hug my hips in a way that made me feel satisfied in my appearance. I decided to splurge and buy all three pieces. Afterall, my rent was paid, I was caught up on all my bills, and I had already paid off my credit card. My column job in New York increased my pay to $5.50 a word, which was amazing considering my actual proximity to the New York nightlife. Regardless of the circumstances, I had the money to go a little crazy if I wanted to. I knew I already had a nice pair of fitted jeans at home that would fit and several pairs of high heeled sandals that made my legs look extra-long and extra lean. With these few new items, I would have all I needed to create a few cute date night outfits if the opportunity presented itself. As I paid for the items and approached the ferry to travel back, I began to wonder how tall Mr. green eyes was. I had guessed 6 feet, but I wasn't certain, and I didn't stand up when he approached. I'm 5 foot 8, so I'm hoping my shoes won't cause me to tower over him. I'd hate not to be lined up with those sexy eyes. Would my heels make me too tall? Is a dress even appropriate for a coffee date? Maybe just the blouse and jeans for the first interaction?

Decisions. Decisions.

At least I had some decisions to make other than choosing white or red to fill my wine glass. And so, I pondered on my options and his height as I watched the waves splash up on the ferry. The sun was starting to set, and the view was breathtaking, as always. It was late Spring and unseasonably warm for the northeastern corner of Maine which typically remained just a touch colder than the rest of the coast in May. The wind blew through my shoulder length brown hair and though it felt nice, I wished I had brought a clip or ponytail holder with me. Never prepared, I thought, but boy wasn't it a beautiful night?

I arrived back home about an hour and 20 minutes later with packages in hand and I felt just a tad bit nervous about everything. I entered my apartment and placed my purchases on the ottoman next to the front door which served as a "catch all" for my things. The apartment was small, but perfect for a single woman. The bedroom had great light. I placed my bed in the direction of the bay window looking out at the quaint downtown skyline. Basically, the two office buildings, *The Beanery*, and a couple of mom-and-pop cafes. It was still quite lovely. I could see the sun come up each morning and I never used blinds or curtains. I liked to rise with the light. The promise of a new day helped with my situational depression and so I arranged things in my life and my living space to encourage this. The sun coming up in the North window brought me that peace. Similarly, the quaint back patio provided peace with beautiful sunsets. When the winter blues hit, the loss of leaves from the trees gave me a small glimpse of the shoreline. It would be perfect for entertaining a small group of friends, and so I decorated the patio as if entertaining would ensue; a small grill, which I obviously do not know how to turn on, so I have yet to use, a small table with chairs, and a smallish firepit with four Adirondack chairs surrounding it. I even installed a sound system so music could be played during the get-togethers. But for now, it was just an area where I quietly read or worked on my column. I did put a small hammock up for relaxing, one that came with a free-standing frame to avoid taking up too much space. It was perfect and I was able to enjoy it myself each evening. And the small table, intended for entertainment, became a quiet retreat to work and write. No, it wasn't used for entertaining just yet, but I was enjoying it. Especially with an occasional glass of wine as I watched the sunsets.

The kitchen was likewise small, but it had beautiful countertops made of granite and enough room in the stove to store extras because I'm not much of a cook. I didn't see the need for a table, as a consistent table for one, but I did buy the cutest high back barstool which I placed in front of the small island situated in the center of the kitchen. I used the stool as a vanity chair and at my desk when writing. It is versatile, and versatility has always been important to me. Through a narrow corridor was a smallish living area where I decided upon an upscale futon instead of a couch; just in case I had any visitors, but that has yet to happen in the over six years I have lived in this small town in Maine. Other than some take out in the fridge and a deluxe wine cooler, I really did not have much use for anything other than my bedroom and patio. I did not even own any real China, just a pot, a skillet, and several plastic plates, cups, and bowls. I did own four wine glasses, because no one appreciates drinking wine out of a plastic cup. I usually used paper products to avoid washing dishes or I just ate right out of the takeout box. I was comfortable with my mundane and independent schedule and life for that matter, but my heart was open...just a little, and I was eager to see where it would take me. I realized in all of the excitement that I had not eaten all day. Here it was almost 8 o'clock at night, and the only thing I had consumed today was coffee and a piece of dry rye toast. I gave *Ollo's Pizza* a ring and ordered my regular: A personal mushroom pizza and a bottle of sweet red. Jess, who had been my delivery person since I moved to town, arrived with my dinner within the usual 35-minute window, and I took the bottle, the pizza, and my glass to the back patio. I sipped my wine and enjoyed each of the four slices of pizza as I listened to a little slow jazz and watched the first few leaves blow on the newly budded trees that surrounded my backyard. Soon the leaves and flowers would be in full bloom, as would everything around me, and the view of the coast would become difficult, but with the welcome of the new season, I felt like I was starting to open and bloom as well, and that was something to celebrate. So, I raised my glass to me and took a drink as I watched the sun go down.

Chapter 7-Mr. Green Eyes

I rolled out of bed with a little more enthusiasm than normal. I wanted to have some extra time to primp before heading out for my coffee date. I stayed up longer than expected last night to try to finish Friday's column, just in case things took a positive turn after our first date...if that's even what it was. My column is based on living in a big city and the attractiveness of being a single gal amid it all. It's pure fiction. And I feel guilty about it. The writing is believable, but I hate living a lie, even if it is considered fiction. I live in this small town with zero-night life and my single life is obviously nothing to brag about, but to be fair, it's been like that since the beginning. I had only worked as a columnist for three months when Max and I decided to elope. If I were to jump on a plane, I could be in the big city in about 9 hours, but with 550 miles between me and the bright lights, my column was starting to struggle. When I first started writing about the nightlife and happenings of NYC, I loved the bigness, and even with living in the suburbs in Jersey, it didn't detract too much from the spontaneity that the city offered. I spent weekends visiting and I still sometimes miss the feel of a crisp newspaper in my hand while taking the A Train to weekly meetings, but once I moved there and was right in the middle of it, I realized the big lights were a distraction from the ugliness that embodied the city. So, I've held on to the positive and try to write of a nightlife I dreamt of or from my past dreams, if you will, and live vicariously through my good memories of the city. The rest is just exaggerated fodder. Amazingly, I am still able to keep up and develop believable content as the words have always come easily on the written page for me. Unfortunately, this is not the case when it comes to making idle conversation. So, my main goal is to keep my ADHD at bay and attempt to have a genuine, two-way conversation with this gorgeous man, though my track record for this is zero. It's so much easier to manage once I have established a relationship with someone and they are aware of my intricacies. Hopefully my positive attributes will wow him enough to overlook the rest.

Once showered, I grabbed the striped blouse from yesterday and buttoned it up over my push up bra. It gave my size B's a boost and made me look almost like a full C. My jeans fit the curves of my ass just perfectly and the heels were brown and strappy. The heels were one of the items in my wardrobe that were faithful; they never let me down. I swooped my hair up into a messy bun because I didn't want to look like I tried too hard for a coffee date, but I curled the loose pieces that framed my face. I added a little modest makeup with a rosy cheek and a light dusty rose lip gloss. I grabbed my favorite necklace, a silver chain with a very small birthstone that my father had given me before he suddenly passed away. I lost him just before I met Max, so I believe some of my attachment to this seemingly gentle man was a result of my yearning for some type of acceptance from a man in lieu of losing my father so prematurely. It usually brought me good luck. And I decided on my dangly silver earrings to accent my hair swooped up. A little spray of perfume in the necessary places; specifically, behind my ears and the back of my neck, trigger spots for me if you will, and I was ready to go. *The Beanery* was just a five-minute walk from my flat and the weather was cooperating today; not too windy, and just warm enough to not need a jacket. I grabbed my purse and headed out the front door, eager to see what Mr. green eyes was

all about.

Chapter 8-The Beanery

I arrived a few minutes ahead of schedule, so I placed my purse on my usual corner table, the one where I met Jeff just two days before, and I went up to the barista to order my caramel latte. I didn't want to be too forward, and I didn't want Jeff to think that he had to buy my coffee, so I ordered a larger size so it would last once he arrived, hopeful that the conversation would outlast the coffee. I sat there sipping and waiting as the clock ticked past nine. At 9:10 Jeff came barreling in. He was loud and clumsy and somehow still charming. He stopped by my table and said, "Can I get you something else while I'm up there? I planned on treatin' you today." I was trying to remain poised and confident, so I smiled and said, "No Thank you. I'm fine with my latte for now."

He nodded and headed up to get a large black coffee, one cream. His voice was deep and boisterous so everyone in the coffee shop knew what he had ordered. Plain and simple. I liked that about him already. He returned with his hot beverage and slid in next to me rather than taking the chair directly across from my seat. Almost shoulder to shoulder Jeff asked, "So what's your story little lady? Or is that too forward?" I giggled a little and I was almost embarrassed for myself. Here I am, 49 years old, giggling and gawking at some grown ass man, again. I felt myself start to put my guard up, but the flattery took over and I continued with just a flushed face and coy smile. I tried to brush my embarrassment off, cleared my throat as a nervous reaction, and said, "Well, I'm a "come here." Jeff giggled and said, "A come here you say? Most of us "from heres" know when you're a come here. Pretty obvious don't ya think?"

The nerve of him, I thought to myself. Everyone here must be an asshole. As if having every female I have interacted with in this little town treat me like an outsider wasn't enough, now this?

My gut told me to get up and leave at once. I mean, who cares if he's just joking? This bullshit is offensive to people who have come to this community and want to add something to the town. I still hadn't responded. I'm not even certain how much time had passed. Then I thought to myself, I am the one that started this when I called myself a "come here." Maybe I was anticipating the reaction and so I subconsciously invited sarcasm. I had learned from my ex, Max, never to anticipate anything! That should have been enough of a warning. I looked up from my cup and said, "I don't think it's that obvious. I was just referring to myself in the way the entire town has been treating me since I moved here six years ago. I'm from New Jersey, close to the New York border. I'm much more of a city girl than you're probably used to. I'm adapting to the small-town lifestyle, primarily because I needed a break and because I love the water, the salt in the air, and the ability to walk just about anywhere I need to go without driving. I guess that's something New York City and this town have in common. Probably the only thing."

Jeff turned sideways in his chair and looked directly into my eyes. Those damn eyes. Sparkling green and so dreamy. I'm certain he could convince me of just about anything without even speaking. He paused as he gazed at me and I felt lost, almost in a trance. He then said, "I knew you were from the city. I've noticed you before. Just took me awhile to get up the nerve to say something. I asked around a bit before I made my move. I knew you frequented *The Beanery* at 9 a.m. on Tuesday mornings. I knew you wrote a column for some NYC newspaper on big city life. I got a hold of a copy and then ordered a subscription about five weeks ago. Been reading it. Interesting stuff. But it's not the life I'm accustomed to and I'm pretty sure it never could be. I guess I was waiting to see if you were staying. I wasn't aware you'd been here for six years, or I would have made my move a little sooner."

I stared in shock and amazement. I wasn't quite sure how I felt. I knew I was intrigued. My taste in men had changed as I had moved into my 40's. The young men just weren't as attractive to me anymore. I didn't care much for abs and muscles. Not as much as a nice beard, a job, and a personality. The beard and personality were on point; I was wondering at this point what he did for a living in this small town, but I wasn't quite comfortable enough to ask. These long pauses were becoming awkward, so I simply smiled and said, "I'm flattered. I really am. I really don't know what to say, but I am glad to meet you."

"I'm hoping to see you more than just today, Alicia. I'd like to have dinner this weekend if you're free. Does Saturday night work for you, or are you even interested?"

I didn't want to seem too excited, so I just said, "I don't have anything planned so that sounds fine to me."

We continued to talk back and forth about small details of our lives and Jeff mentioned that he had worked for the *Fary Banks Lighthouse* for 25 years and had recently retired a little early. At 55 years of age, Jeff was financially stable, retired with plenty of free time, and very interested in me. He was a little older than I had expected; I had never even considered a man older than 50, but I was already charmed by him. And I guess since I was nearing the half century point myself, I should probably start increasing the scope of age in my dating pool.

I tried to contain my enthusiasm and just nod and smile as he spoke, but I was struggling. It was the first time in years that I had felt anything for anyone, and it was about damn time.

Chapter 9-About Damn Time

Jeff offered to walk me home after the coffee. We walked down Main Street and past the park. As we made a right towards my flat, Jeff reached down to grab my hand. It felt natural for some odd reason, so I didn't fight it. It had been so long since I had held someone's hand, much less anything else, I embraced the attention. As we approached my front door, I became nervous and wasn't sure what to do. It was barely noon on a Thursday, and it seemed like such an odd time to end a date. I couldn't ask him in for coffee because obviously, that was the entire first date to begin with. I lied and said I had to work on my column for tomorrow to try and ward off some of the awkwardness; he smiled and said he figured as much. As I reached for my keys in my purse, Jeff gently reached up and touched my right cheek. He then leaned in and gently kissed me, one little peck, on my lips. He then stepped back and said, "I'll see you Saturday night at five darlin. I have several things planned." I smiled and nodded and stepped into my apartment. As he walked away, I hustled to my bedroom to watch him from the bay window. It was at this point that I realized we had not even exchanged phone numbers. I didn't even ask what his last name was. Finally, anticipation meant something to me again, and for a change, it wasn't a negative emotion.

It was only Thursday afternoon and I had lots of time between now and Saturday to overthink. Thankfully I already had a plan for my outfit; the dress I picked up at *The Plaza* in preparation for the coffee date. I was excited to have something to look forward to for a change. I hadn't found a new girlfriend to gossip with or have lunch with, but I did have a promising plan with someone soon, and I couldn't help but be overjoyed about it. I walked to my closet and pulled out the light blue dress I had already hung up after returning home from shopping, and I began rustling through the pile of shoes on the floor. I didn't want to have to resort to the same strappy sandals I was wearing today; after all, variety is the spice of life, so I dug through the pile to find my alternate brown shoes, a short-heeled pair of espadrilles. They were casual and comfortable, but just dressy enough not to take away from the blue cotton dress. I grabbed the shoes and placed them beside the dress and then went to my jewelry box to find something right to accessorize with. My jewelry box had belonged to my grandmother, and it was my prized possession. The only thing that mirrored its significance was the necklace that my father gave me, which I gently took off and placed on one of the three hooks in grandma's jewelry box. I decided to keep things casual and grabbed my silver beaded necklace and matching dangly earrings. I was content with the plan and hung the jewelry next to the dress and shoes in my closet and shut the door. I looked at my watch and realized that not only was it already two in the afternoon, but I had only had coffee and nothing to eat. This was becoming a regular occurrence for me; definitely something I needed to work on. I needed to get to the gym down the street to get in a quick workout so I decided to grab something to eat on the way; that would leave plenty of time this evening to overthink all of the intricacies of Saturday night.

I changed out of my jeans and new top into a pair of gym shorts and a modest sports bra. I tossed my strappy sandals onto the floor next to my bed and tied up my running shoes. My gym bag was always packed and lying on the ottoman next to the front door. I grabbed my wallet and keys from my purse and then tossed them into the gym bag and headed out the door. As I began the ten-minute-walk towards the village gym, I observed things about the small town that I hadn't noticed before. Most of the onlookers were smiling. Did they always smile and look welcoming, or was today just a special day? The storefronts were nicely decorated and beamed with a "Welcome Spring" glow I hadn't noticed before. Just minutes to the gym I decided to stop in the local café, *Sammie's and Such* to grab a quick bite. After ordering a turkey pita and a side of fresh fruit, I found a small table close to the window. I sat down and looked out in amazement of just how pretty Fary banks was. For some reason the sun was shining especially bright today, and I felt a sense of peace I hadn't felt in such a long time. I took a sip of my Diet soda and simply smiled. Today was the beginning of the new me...or at least the beginning of

a new perspective on life for me. I decided that even

if Mr. Green Eyes and I didn't work out, I was still

going to try my darndest to find the silver lining here

in Fary banks.

Chapter 10-Finally, Saturday

The last day and a half of the week seemed to drag on and on. I was so happy to fall asleep and arrive on Saturday morning. I was ready to see Jeff again and see where this might lead. I decided to get up early and make myself a cup of coffee and enjoy it with the sunrise in the bay window of my bedroom. It had a small platform, so on chilly days I could lie on the windowsill with a pillow and blanket and read or write or simply just stare out at the beauty of the small town on a crisp morning. It wasn't crisp or even remotely chilly, but I still wanted to take advantage of this time to sit, reflect, and enjoy my cup of joe. I was already seeing things differently, more clearly. I was beginning to realize that maybe my inhibitions were preventing me from making friends in this small town rather than everyone just avoiding me or finding me uninteresting. Apparently, all it took to help me come to this realization was a tall, dark, handsome man named Jeff...with a beard and sparkling green eyes of course. Those eyes. Pretty much still all I could think about. I continued to sip my morning courage when I heard my phone ring. I stumbled up from the sill to grab it off my bed and a new number was displayed on the ID. It was a local 734-area code, but the number wasn't familiar. Honestly, besides the local carryout numbers, I really didn't know anyone's number in the 734-area code. After about three rings I decided to brave it and answer.

"Hello, this is Alicia." A deeper voice replied, "Mornin' darlin. Hope you don't find this too forward, but I stopped in the local pizza place and sweet talked the owner into giving me your number. I realized after I left on Thursday that I didn't ask you for it and I wanted to hear your voice."

My heart smiled as did my face, and my cheeks were already starting to hurt a little. I was child-like embarrassed and so thankful he couldn't see me blushing through the phone.

"Good morning, Jeff. I realized the same, but I'm not quite as crafty as you are in my undercover strategies." We both laughed and I continued speaking. "I figured we'd just exchange numbers tonight if everything went well. I am glad that you called though. I must admit I've been thinking about you quite a bit these past few days."

It seemed easier to be honest behind the safety of my telephone so I decided that I would say exactly what I was thinking about, even if I did regret it later tonight. When he asked me questions, I answered, honestly. I saw no point in pretending I wasn't attracted to him or interested. We spoke for roughly 15 minutes about really nothing at all, which was kind of nice for a change. It felt like old friends chatting, and boy did I need that! I was doing my darndest to stay focused and to drink him in. I was determined to slow down and stay present in the moment, but it was a real struggle for me. Having my heartbroken like I have, combined with my inability to control my attention for any length of time, was sure to hurt my chances with Jeff, but I was going to try with everything in my power. Listening to him speak seemed to feed my soul. It was like watering a parched plant; he fed me, hydrated me, and I was slowly coming back to life. If just a brief phone conversation could make me feel this way, what would several hours tonight do? Would I be able to remain in control if necessary? I just wasn't sure, and honestly, I wasn't certain if I even cared. I was ready to jump.

After we said goodbye for now, I finished up my coffee and threw on my gym clothes. I wanted to get a workout in and still have time for plenty of fussing over myself this afternoon. I started the walk towards the village gym when my phone rang again. I grabbed my gym bag on the way out the door and answered the strange number.

"Hello, this is Alicia." The voice on the other line was a woman. She had a very quiet voice; mousy like.

"Hello, Alicia. You don't know me, but sadly I know of you. I know you from Jeff. I mean Jeff knows you apparently and Jeff is my husband. My name is Shelly. Shelly Linford. Mrs. Jeff Linford."

My thoughts raced and I wasn't even sure I could comprehend what she was saying. Surely to God this man, this seemingly perfect man, isn't married. I refuse to be the "other" woman. Especially after what I had been through with Max. Maybe it was a different Jeff she was referring to. I didn't even know his last name. It was totally possible that she was mistaken and didn't know of me at all.

I responded hesitantly, "Your husband? I'm not sure I know who your husband is."

She responded with a little more emphasis in her voice this time.

"Yes, you most certainly do. I believe you have a date with him this evening, or at least that is what he is telling me. Look, I know he likes the ladies. I'm aware of many of his indiscretions. He plays around with someone for a while, gets bored, and then returns home to me. I know this about him, and I have been putting up with his charades for quite some time, but I fear this time he may be taking it a little too far. I know he has been pursuing you, at least quietly, for the last few months. He knows more about you, I believe, than he does about me after all these years. Our relationship is purely plutonic. We're not sexual anymore; we just get each other, and the friendship is too important to me to allow his escapades with other women to split us up indefinitely. I want to be clear. I'm not threatening you. I'm not jealous. I'm just concerned that one or both of you may get hurt. Especially if you are not privy to this information already."

As I listened to Shelly speak, I couldn't help but feel sorry for her. It seemed she was in love with a man who could not love her back, and I was all too familiar with this scenario. In the same vein, this could be good news for me, but do I really want to fall in love with a man who can't love me back either? Again?

I could tell by her words and her tone that I liked her. My mind slipped away from the date with Jeff and began wondering what would happen if I just dropped old green eyes all together and maybe just met Shelly for a drink. Could we be friends? It sounds ridiculous, but I could tell she too was lonely and needed someone to talk to.

After a long pause I replied, "Shelly, I am very sorry that you have been put in this position. I truly did not know. I do like him. If I'm being honest, he's all I have thought about this week until this conversation."

Shelly broke into my words before I could finish another sentence. "Alicia, honestly, I am fine with the arrangement. I'm just not sure you will be. Those before you were not, and the fact that you have not discussed this with him yet is concerning, or rather, he has not discussed it with you."

I was trying to muster up the right reaction. "To be completely forthcoming, we haven't spent enough time together to share any intimate details so I really should give Jeff the benefit of the doubt. I understand your arrangement, but I do not want to cause any more heartache for you. Would it be awkward if we met for a drink sometime and maybe discussed it a little more?"

Shelly paused. She wasn't sure herself how to react to this. This was new territory for her for sure. Shelly decided that maybe this would be beneficial. After all, she really didn't have any friends here since her best friend passed aways six years prior. Other than Jeff, she spent most of her time alone. She had closed the door to friendships because the pain was so unbearable losing Julie and she believed deep down she held on to Jeff so she wouldn't be completely and utterly alone. Shelly responded, "You know what, Alicia, I think this sounds like a good idea. How's Tuesday evening, say six at *Annie's Bar?*

"Sounds good," Alicia said reluctantly. "I'll see you then. And for now, let's just keep this relationship stuff between us. I am going on the date with Jeff tonight, but I'm not certain where it will take any of us."

"Understood," and don't spend your evening worrying about me. I'm good, I promise. I just felt compelled to tell you. From what Jeff has said, you're a real nice gal. I'd hate to see you get hurt. Talk to you soon, Alicia."

"Talk to you soon, Shelly, and thanks for the heads up."

Now completely disoriented, I sat my gym bag back down and just dropped to the floor. What am I going to do now? Obviously, I need to go on this date, but honestly all I could think about was Shelly. It was awkward, but she could potentially be a real friend. I mean she seems lonely. I'm lonely. It wouldn't work as a triangle, and I'm sure this drink is just a formality so she can check me out a little closer and convince me that Jeff is no good for me. And what about Jeff? Would he even tell me? If he does, how does he expect me to react? I mean what kind of woman dates a married man knowingly? A whore does, and that's not me, that's for certain.

I decided to skip the gym and I was too nervous to eat, so I made me another cup of coffee and retreated to my window. I looked out and wondered what to do next. At least there was a next and that was something to still be happy about whether it be with Jeff or a new friend, however awkward it may seem.

Chapter 11-Just in Time

Jeff arrived at the door right at five o'clock, and I was more than ready. He knocked three times fast and I opened the door with a childlike grin on my face. My dimples were obvious, I'm certain, as they are kind of my trademark. That and long legs of course. I suppose my kind heart and my intellect should be noted ahead of physical characteristics, but men do not often notice those attributes first, and women tend to focus on whatever parts of them offer a competitive edge.

He smiled back and said, "You look ready darlin.' Let's head out. "

I nodded, still silly smiling, and we took off on foot to what I believed to be a dinner reservation.

That was probably the nicest aspect of this small town. You could walk just about anywhere. We walked side by side, close enough to hold hands, but not comfortable enough to at this point. Though it didn't stop him on the way home from the coffee shop, I believed that was more of a kindness than a dating ploy to ease my nerves. We passed the pizza joint, and *The Beanery*, and I giggled quietly to myself at the thought of how all of this started just days ago in this very spot. I've always been a big person for signs and following my arrow. Whichever way my arrow took me, I followed. But should my arrow be leading me in this direction? I was so taken by his presence and the excitement of a plan that I had almost forgotten about Shelly. I decided to just let things be and wait for him to share the details of his odd marital arrangement. And if nothing came to surface by the end of the date, I would have to bring it up myself, especially considering my upcoming plans with her.

As we walked, we spoke of our past and I mentioned Daddy and grandma; he shared his life at the lighthouse and that he had an ex-wife that he didn't really interact with much anymore.

Hmm, I thought to myself. No mention of Shelly directly, and divorced?

Someone was lying, but I didn't want him to know about my conversation behind his back with her, so I just listened. At least for now. And honestly, I hadn't done anything wrong. I didn't reach out to her. I didn't give her any information. I just tentatively planned to meet up with her and there was still time to cancel that plan if I really wanted to.

Jeff continued telling me about his life and I loved that he trusted me enough to share these details. At least some of them anyway. No children, which was a relief to me after what I had went through with Max early on in our marriage, and he explained that he had several investment properties he was managing. He was a flipper: He bought and flipped houses as added income during retirement, and it had proven quite profitable for him. I wanted to mention Max, but I was hesitant. He was a bad part of my past and I didn't want it to taint my immediate future. I planned on telling him when the time was right.

I felt like we really understood each other. It's odd how sometimes you just click with people. And we clicked. About 20 minutes into our walk, we arrived at *Anna's Bar and Bistro*. Jeff approached the host with our reservation, and he walked us to a private table for two in the back corner of the restaurant. A wine bottle and two glasses had already been delivered and the table was lit by candle. Jeff pulled out my chair and before sitting, he poured me a glass of the house red wine. Not too fancy, but a sweet gesture. I sipped and fiddled with the menu in front of me. I hated ordering, especially on a first date. He eliminated my anxiety over this by saying, " I hope you don't mind, but I took the liberty of ordering for us when I made the reservation. I knew it might be a little forward, but I thought it might be exciting for us to try something new since we're new as well. "

I was relieved and nodded approvingly, only hoping he didn't order something like escargot or liver. Minutes later a lovely cheese plate arrived with French bread and an assortment of crackers. I nibbled on the variety and smiled and nodded while he continued to share intimate details about his life. I wasn't as forthcoming, but I continued to give him little snippets to keep the conversation flowing. The courses of food continued to come including a spring mix salad with a house vinaigrette, a lobster tail paired with a small filet mignon and seasonal vegetables and whipped potatoes. It was a beautiful meal and all so delicious. I loved every bite and I felt comfortable, at ease with Jeff, even while eating, which was a first for me. Another peeve of mine is that I dislike eating in front of someone I don't know, especially if it's a male who seems interested in me, but Jeff continued to put my mind at ease.

As the server cleared the dinner dishes, a jazz band began to start their set. People slowly parted their tables and began dancing. "Can I have this dance?" Jeff snickered and stood up and reached his arms out to touch mine.

 "Well, I suppose you can, though I don't know if I can move after all of this food." I stood up and he took my hand to lead me to the dance floor. It felt odd to have my hand in his, though I knew it was just a formality to lead the lady to the floor. We danced cheek to cheek at first. I guess it was easier than making eye contact. The music was slow, and the harmony was invigorating. The act of dancing this close to him gave me a feeling I hadn't experienced in a while, and it embarrassed me a little bit. As the next tune sped up a little, we separated our faces and stepped back into a traditional dance position. Jeff held my hands up to support his frame and we began dancing more formally, as if we were waltzing. "I am having a wonderful time, Alicia. This is the first time I have felt this way in years. Like a kid again. Excited to see what comes next."

I just nodded and smiled, but I knew he could tell I was feeling it too.

We danced to several more songs until the band took a break. He grabbed my hand, but again, and led me back to our corner table. As soon as we arrived, the server brought us after dinner cappuccinos and a slice of cheesecake. Just one slice with two forks. At this point I was feeling comfortable, so I grabbed the fork closest to me and sliced a piece of the cake off. It was so creamy and delicious and together we ate every bite. After dessert we decided that we'd had enough dancing and so we left *Anna's* and headed towards the beach.

This was perfect, I thought to myself. I love the beach, the waves, the salt in the air, the sand beneath my toes, the entire experience. As we stood on the beach, under the moonlight, quite possibly the most cliché thing ever described, but truly one of the most romantic evenings I had ever experienced, I wondered how this woman, Shelly, could be so comfortable with this wonderful man being with other women. There had to be a flaw.

Maybe I deserve more, I thought to myself. Maybe this is me being so starved for attention that I am overplaying how wonderful this date has been...this week...this man.

I could accept this date as just a one-time thing and enjoy it for what it was, and search for something more, with less potential strings, but the concept of more has always left me astray. I mean I can always find more, but I could just as easily end up with less, and he made me feel full. I'm making room for all the things I think I deserve. To do that, I needed to be willing to let go of all the things I'd been storing in my mind that's been taking up space, rent free. And whatever Shelly's story was, she wasn't living here in my mind tonight. Her story didn't necessarily have to be my story, just as my previous story with Max didn't need to be an encore. I continued to live in the moment and drink him in.

At the end of the most wonderful evening, kissing me good night seemed pointless. We had been kissing and holding each other on the beach for hours. We acted like two school kids in love, and it was only date number two. So, I took a leap of faith and asked him if he wanted to come in. To my surprise, he declined. Was it because of me, something I said or did? Or was he just trying to be a gentleman?

"Darlin," I have an early meeting tomorrow over a contract for another property. I need to get some rest, but would you like to meet for breakfast afterwards?

"Sure," I said, with a little disappointment. How about you stop by and get me after your meeting?"

"Sounds good darlin.' See you around 10 in the morning. I had a wonderful time."

As he turned away to leave, I didn't know if I wanted to smile or cry. Things seemed so great, but there was still the cloud of Shelly floating over my head and we had yet to discuss it. I felt so overwhelmed with emotion; some happy, but more inquisitive than anything. I was already falling, and I was falling hard.

Chapter 12-Sunday Morning Comes

After a good night's sleep, I got up and had my usual

coffee and then unlocked my front door before

getting in the shower. I wanted to make sure Jeff

could get in if I didn't hear him, and for some

reason, I trusted him to do so. It was a sunny

morning with a light breeze, so I left the window

open in the screen door. I could smell the freshly

bloomed flowers and hear the birds chirping. The

morning was surreal. Just lovely. I headed to the

shower and started lathering up when I heard a loud,

unsettling noise from the kitchen. Someone,

hopefully Jeff, had busted through the door allowing

the screen door to slam back and forth in the wind. I

thought it to be a little forward of him, especially

since he didn't know where I was in the apartment. I

was in the shower and the sound startled me, but

excited me at the same time. I knew it was him, and I

didn't care anymore that Shelly might still be in the picture. I'd spent most of the night tossing and turning over it, and I'd come to the conclusion that my happiness needed to come first. My feelings were weaved between the forces of right and wrong, but my desire for him was stronger, and I had relinquished any thought of doing what was right at this point. I wanted him. I wanted to feel good, and I had made up my mind that feeling good was right.

He slipped quietly through the narrow corridor to my bedroom. It was odd that he came in with such force and then grew so silent. I walked out of the bathroom with a towel draped over the bottom half of my body. I didn't bother to dry myself off. Water gently dripped from my breasts and though it was warm from the dampness of the shower, my nipples were erect. I was clearly excited about whatever was about to take place and the anticipation was almost enough to kill me. Suddenly I couldn't breathe. I gasped for breath as he made his way through my door and towards me. He grabbed the towel nestled around my hips and tossed it to the floor. It wasn't gentle. It whipped across my skin and stung a little. Fully dressed, he cupped his hands around my hips and lifted me to his waist. There I was, completely exposed and wrapped around his clothed body. He began to kiss my neck and behind my ears. These two spots literally drove me crazy, and apparently, he knew it. Maybe he'd noticed the attention I paid to these areas with my perfume. I wasn't sure, but I liked it and so did he. He tossed me back on to my unmade bed and began kissing parts of me that hadn't been touched in quite some time. I wanted to tell him to stop, but I just couldn't. This one-sided foreplay continued for what felt like hours, but probably lasted only minutes. When I thought I couldn't take much more, he paused, sat up slowly, and removed his shirt. I sat up partially and took note of his chest which was broad and muscular. Age had not affected his strength or build and apparently his desire to take charge. I was certain he could manage chopping wood or wrangling a bull, something manly and strong like that. The thought of that made me giggle a little and though he noticed my snicker, he kept going. We were so in sync that he probably knew what I was thinking and therefore wasn't distracted by it.

He had little sprouts of gray chest hair that I found to be oddly sexy. I noticed a small scar just above his nipple on the left side of his chest. A badge of courage I'm certain. I took my index finger and gently stroked the marking. I then reached towards the button on his jeans. They were torn and tethered, and I felt like I was opening something exquisite; a gift just for me.

He stared deeply into my eyes with that green, piercing glow and I just knew he could see straight through me. He continued to lock eyes with me and began caressing my cheek as I unzipped his pants. He slid his jeans the rest of the way off and continued to undress until we were both completely vulnerable and anxiously awaiting the next step. I laid back on my own, retreating, and ready. He moved forward and leaned into me. He made love to me in a way I had never experienced before. He took his time. I was his only focus. My pleasure. My contentment. And once we were through, I knew, in that moment, I'd never be able to let him go.

It wasn't just chemistry.

It wasn't just about convenience.

It was a soul attraction. We made sense and I could feel it in places I had never felt it before. His light healed me. His touch made me believe again. He understood all of me...my mind, body, and soul. He needed no direction and that alone made me yearn for him even more.

Finally, my suffering had some meaning. It was my path to Jeff. I had to experience pain to appreciate his love. But I also knew that if Shelly was still in the picture, this feeling would soon take on another meaning. More heartache. More misery. More pain. Still, I was going to relish in the afterglow of this love making and not allow anyone or anything to ruin it for me.

This moment. This moment was here, and I was going to take it. It doesn't matter what might be. All that matters is what we did with this very moment in time. And as far as I was concerned, that was enough.

I felt compelled to ask just one question, even though I really did want to say anything at all out of fear of tainting the moment. Afterall, I was perfectly content with just lying in his arms for a while. My lips were chapped, aching, but in a way that let me know I was breakfast, and we probably weren't eating anything at all. Oddly, I was fine with that. That ache is one that you yearn for.

So, I asked, "Jeff, what is your last name?"

"It's Linford, Alicia. Jeff Linford."

I quietly whispered the words, "Alicia Linford? I kind of like the sound of that."

And for the rest of the morning, we just existed in each other's arms. Motionless and content until we both drifted off to sleep.

After sleeping for several hours, we both woke up feeling refreshed and satisfied, at least I did. I gave Jeff a brief tour of the small flat that I called home. I brewed a fresh pot of coffee and we escaped to the back patio where we continued to snuggle and sip our coffee in silence. It was the most at peace I had felt in years. And I prayed it was just the beginning of many more breakfast dates for the two of us.

After several hours, Jeff got dressed and headed out for a meeting for another house on the outskirts of Fary Banks, and I didn't even think to ask when I would see him again. It felt more like a couple separating for work for the day with the intent of a return once the night fell. He softly kissed my lips, gave me a wink, and left.

Chapter 13- The Ex-Mrs. Jack Linford

I spent most of Monday writing and searching for a new gig. This New York bullshit was too much for me now. It felt fake and unfamiliar, and I wanted to find a way to blend my life here with my writing career. I had no luck with the search unfortunately, but there was time. My contract for the New York column was active until September. Hopefully I can come up with enough material to hold interest until then. Tuesday came around and Jeff called to tell me good morning. I was so preoccupied with my work search that it didn't even occur to me to be troubled over not seeing or hearing from him Monday evening. I also did not feel any desire to push when things were going as well as they were in just a few short days. I was becoming quite comfortable with him and looking forward to hearing his voice. I couldn't help but wonder if this was a bad thing.

Being happy changes things. You start to want more. You even expect it. And tonight, after secretly meeting with Shelly, our relationship might change completely. But I felt I owed it to all three of us to meet her and at least hear her out.

Around 5:30 p.m. I started towards *Annie's Bar* which conveniently was the Bistro Jeff and I had just enjoyed a romantic dinner at on Saturday. When I arrived, I noticed a short, blonde-haired woman, probably in her early 50's sitting at the bar alone. She was sipping on what appeared to be a martini and she was dressed like someone who had plenty of money. Her hair was short and was turned under neatly so that it framed her chin. She wore dainty little glasses, and her accessories weren't cheapy silver chains and costume dangly earrings. She wore diamonds. Large diamonds, and I could see them boldly glimmering from the entryway of the bar. I slowly approached and once there I tapped her on the shoulder. "Shelly? Shelly Linford?"

She turned around and smiled. "Yes, you must be Alicia. Sorry, I don't believe I ever did get your last name. What is it dear?"

"Edwards. Alicia Edwards. Nice to meet you."

Shelly continued the conversation; I assume to avoid awkwardness. "Do you want a drink, Alicia? Maybe a Cosmo or a martini? No wait, you're a wine girl. Sweet red I believe is what I heard. Bartender, could I get a fresh martini, and could my friend here get a glass of your finest sweet red?"

"Thank you," I said shyly. I do love wine." So, what should we talk about? I admit I am intrigued by you and your situation, but I must be honest, I do find Jeff to be exquisite and I am starting to fall for him already. So, if there's more that I need to know, sooner is better than later."

As soon as the words left my mouth, I began to regret them. I probably didn't want to know what she was about to tell me, and it wouldn't matter anyway. I'm already in too deep. If after knowing Jeff for only a week made me feel like this, what would happen in a month? Shelly smiled and began spilling all sorts of tea.

"Well, Alicia, as I said before, Jeff really likes the ladies. All types. All sizes. Doesn't seem to have a preference. Usually, it's just informal encounters: A drink or a quick lunch and some random one-night stands. He usually gets in and gets out and that's why our arrangement has always worked, but I was concerned by the amount of research he did on you. It started to feel like maybe this was a bit more serious and so I felt compelled to reach out to you."

Rolling my eyes just enough that I felt better about the bullshit coming out of her mouth, but not enough that she would notice, I worked up a response.

"So, Shelly, what you're telling me is that he's not available? In that you're comfortable with him fooling around, but not having an intimate connection with another woman. And what's even more disturbing about this conversation is that he mentioned you, as his ex-wife, and even stated that he didn't interact with you anymore. He didn't elaborate at all. Just acknowledged that you exist. Seems a little off to me."

Shelly chugged the rest of her martini and stood up from the bar. She leaned in towards my chair and whispered, "Watch your back, Bitch. I was trying to be nice about this, but just know, he will NEVER leave me. EVER! You're nothing more than the flavor of the week, maybe the month, and I decided to warn you about our arrangement to save you from any undue heartache. The way he was speaking of you had me concerned for you, not him...not us, but screw it. If you're this stupid, have at it. It won't end well. I can promise you that!"

Maintaining control so I didn't haul off and throat punch her, I responded confidently and without care for her ignorance and her threats.

"Shelly, it's all fine and well. I'm not intimidated by you and I'm not in competition with you either. I'll have a talk with Jeff, and we will decide together what to make of this bullshit that you're throwing at me. I'd rather hoped we could be friends. I needed a few here in this small town, but not one that acts like you."

I took one more sip of my glass of wine and tossed a $20 on the bar, grabbed my purse, and stormed out.

I didn't look back and I most certainly didn't let her get out ahead of me or get in the last word. It was done for tonight, but this wasn't over.

As I was walking home, I felt confused about the swoosh of emotions I was feeling. Who the Hell does this woman think she is? My intention was to befriend her, but even if she wasn't crazy, why in the world would I think that would be a good idea? Even if what she said is true, Jeff would be mortified if he knew I was plotting something with his wife or his ex-wife or whatever she is to him. My heart wanted to just play pretend and continue with this affair of sorts with Jeff, but my mind created a very different reaction to deal with.

Once home, I bypassed the wine and went straight for the vodka in my freezer. I poured a small amount in a glass and shot it quickly. Then a second. And a third. Soon I no longer cared about Shelly or Jeff or anything else for that matter. I dropped pieces of my clothing off as I headed to the bedroom. I grabbed a bottle of red from the wine cooler and uncorked it and carried it with me. I was beyond needing a glass. With a trail of clothing following me into the room I dropped onto my bed, laid back, and began to drift off, bottle in hand. I was almost asleep when my phone rang. I leaned off the side of my bed to see if I could reach my phone. Apparently, I had dropped it on the floor along with my clothing. It rang a 3rd time and I stumbled to my knees and crawled across the floor to catch the call on the 5th ring. I managed a muffled "Hello."

"Hey there, Darlin,' everything okay?" It was Jeff, dammit. And I was in no position to respond. I knew if I started to speak, I'd emotionally vomit things I couldn't take back, but I just couldn't stop myself.

"No Jeff, everything isn't okay. Let's talk...talk about...oh, never mind."

"Alicia, talk about what? Should I come over?"

"No! Just wait. Let's talk about Shelly."

A long, quite deliberate pause and several heavy breaths came from Jeff's side of the line.

"Jeff? Say something. Say anything. But don't just sit there breathing and whatever else it is that you're doing."

"Okay. I'll talk. I'll explain, Alicia, but I'm coming over."

"It's not a good idea Jeff. I'm drunk. Obliterated. And my defenses are down; I don't want to be in this state of mind and then fall into your arms by default."

While preparing my next argument in my head as to why he couldn't come to my apartment, Jeff said, "I'm here, open up."

Then I heard knocking on my door. I couldn't remember if I had locked it, and I was in no position to drag myself in there to check. Three more knocks and Jeff said, "I'm coming in." He hung up the phone and apparently opened the door because I heard both the screen door and front door slam behind him. He made his way to my room and found me on the floor, clenching the bottle of wine in one hand and my phone in the other. At some point I had slid off the bed without even realizing it. He bent down and took the phone and bottle out of my hands and placed them on the nightstand next to my bed. He then wrapped his arms around and under me and lifted me up and gently placed me back on the bed. I tried to speak, but no words came out, just blubbering and tears. He nuzzled in next to me and held me in his arms. I snuggled my head into the crevice between his arm and chest. I wanted to sit up and scream. I had so much to say, but I was exhausted, mentally and physically, not to mention drunk, and it felt good just to rest my head close to his heart. It felt good to have someone hold me.

He whispered, "We'll talk in the morning," and he reached over and turned off the lamp. I fell asleep in his arms, and in that moment, I felt happy and safe, so I accepted the comfort, at least for tonight.

I woke with the sun like most mornings, but I didn't rush to get out of bed. My head was pounding, and I needed coffee badly, but I was still trying to soak up a few more minutes close to Jeff before the fighting ensued. Jeff rolled over and his green eyes made direct contact with mine, but subconsciously I was telling myself, don't melt into them, Alicia, full knowing it was a losing battle. He leaned in closer and kissed me, softly. I kissed him back. I didn't want to, or I wanted to...or I just didn't know what I wanted.

"Jeff STOP! We need to talk first."

Jeff leaned back just enough to deadlock his eyes on me again, and said, "Okay, Alicia, you deserve the truth, but first, let's make some coffee."

Jeff made a pot of coffee and brought me in a cup. It was curiously strong, not the way I like it, but I suppose I needed the extra jolt after the night I had. I moved over to the bay window and nuzzled up with a blanket. There was dew on the window, and I wiped it away so I could see the sun shining down on the city. Jeff sat down beside me and began to speak.

"Okay, Alicia, let me explain. Shelly is my ex-wife. We divorced over 30 years ago. We were just kids.

Hell, we were only married for four years, but she has caused a lifetime of drama. We do not live together. We do not spend time together. She checks in from time to time, but that's it. She's still in love with me, but we couldn't make it work. We had a child and we lost her when she was a year old. It changed us. We tried counseling. We tried having another child but struggled. It just wasn't working and then she became vindictive. She blamed me for the loss. She blamed me for not being able to have another child. And she resented my work. One week on and one week off was trying on our relationship. So eventually we just gave up. And we're better for it, but her jealousy over my romantic interests always destroys anything I start, but not this time. I'll handle it, Alicia, but you must trust me."

I pondered the information he had just shared, and Shelly was a victim of circumstance and Jeff was obviously still mourning the loss of his child. I understood this pain, but not to the same extent, and I didn't think sharing my experience would improve anything for either of us. I had not even shared the depth of my marriage and divorce to Max with Jeff, so who am I to criticize anything at this point? Still, the almost feral side that sadly exists in every woman was furious, ready to attack, even if it was no fault of Jeff. So, I took a breath and a moment to collect myself, which was no easy feat with this pounding hangover-induced headache, but I managed to just whisper, "I'm not sure what to say."

Jeff nodded in agreement and said, "Then just say nothing and come back to bed."

We crawled back in bed and made love for the second time. It wasn't quite as exciting as our first time together; the anticipation effect had been eliminated, but it was good, and it was exactly what both of us needed at that moment.

Soon after, he left to go find Shelly to have the "necessary" conversation. I was hopeful he could manage it and that we would have an opportunity to build on what we had started together, though we obviously hadn't even had a chance to discuss whatever this is between us. I wasn't sure that I fully trusted his truth. All I knew is that I felt safe in his arms and in his presence. He made me feel full in a town where I'd felt empty for so long. I brewed another pot of coffee and added a little cream and sweetener this time and plopped back down in the window ledge. I just needed time to reflect and think. Normally I would use times like this to get my thoughts down on paper. After all, I have another column due in less than two days, and I hadn't even started it. I was doubting the small-town love affair and the pining ex-wife story would make good New York City nightlife fodder. So, instead of writing, I just sat there.

Jeff was only gone but a couple of hours when my phone rang. I had accomplished absolutely nothing, and it wasn't even a weekend, so my ADHD began kicking in full force. It's all or nothing with me, no gray area, and my mind was leaning strongly towards nothing.

"Hello."

"Hey Darlin' could you meet Shelly and I for a drink at *Anna's* around 6? I want to confront her with you present so we can nip this now. I planned on heading to her apartment, but I didn't want to give her the wrong impression, so I called her and asked her if she'd like to meet me, and she immediately agreed. I'm sure she thinks she's convinced you. She doesn't know you're coming so I'm certain she'll show. "

I didn't want to see her again, but I wanted Jeff, so I decided the sacrifice was worth it.

"Yes, I'll meet you, but I'd be lying if I said I wasn't uncomfortable. We're so new. I have big feelings for you already, but before I start a turf war with your ex, I guess I need to know how serious you are."

"Alicia, I'm a free spirit. I've learned not to commit unless, I'm sure. Usually by the time I've figured out what I want in a relationship the gal has done turned crazy and I'm glad that I didn't fully commit early on. There's something different about you; different about us. I think I'm ready to make the leap, but we need to handle this first; otherwise, you'll never trust me and then we're doomed from the start."

Chapter 14- Confronting "Mrs." Linford

Around 4:00 p.m. I had to drag myself into the bathroom to take a shower. I could still smell Jeff's cologne on me, and I half hated to wash it off. Once I finished cleaning myself up, I grabbed something from the floor of my closet to wear; for a change, I was less than concerned about what I was going to wear or how I would look. This was probably an important opportunity to look nice and to try to prove that I'm worthy of Jeff's admiration, but I just couldn't make myself care enough. Plus, I obviously still felt like shit after the vodka bombs and wine.

I dried my hair and straightened it and brushed a little powder on my face. I grabbed my gloss from the top of my dresser and after putting a little on, I threw it in my purse by the door. I still had an hour before the confrontation, so I decided to crack open my last bottle of red and have a few drinks first. I opened the fridge to find something to nibble on because again, I had apparently forgotten to eat. I thought to myself, as I rummaged through several outdated Chinese food containers, who the Hell forgets to eat? Nobody but me.

I nibbled on some lo Mein noodles and a fortune cookie while I tipped back my glass of wine. After cracking open the cookie I held up the fortune to get a better look. It read, "Peace comes from within. Look for it inside yourself."

Well, that's ironic, I thought to myself. Then I flipped it to read my "lucky numbers." 16, 33, 25, 46, 19, 24. Maybe I should play the lottery. My luck must change soon! Then I focused a bit. I poured a second glass of red. "33." 33 was my Angel number. I believed it followed me; series of threes ever since my daddy passed away. Maybe this was a good sign. He's watching out for me in this situation too. I suddenly felt more comfortable and confident. I decided to put on my red lipstick to snazzy up my look a little, then grabbed my purse and headed to the bar. I can do this. I just need to hold my head up and be honest with Jeff, myself, and my heart.

The evening had a glow about it. The sun was slowly going down and the moon was already abreast. It was as if two light sources were guiding me simultaneously, and I couldn't shake the idea that Daddy was here with me. There were always signs and I appreciated them when they surfaced. I needed them to feel whole on days when I felt empty. I didn't really have a very close relationship with my mother as she left when I was quite young. She'd resurface sporadically, but not for long enough to make a difference. As an only child, other than Daddy, I really didn't have anyone except Max, and Max often was the same as having no one at all. So, this opportunity to actually have a shot at real love and companionship seemed oddly significant. I just didn't want to oversell it in my own mind before I knew for sure what it was. All I knew for certain was that I was engaged by this man and his presence, and I owed it to myself to see what we could be.

I arrived at the bar and paused before walking through the doors. You can do this, I reassured myself again. Upon entering I could hear the slow jazz music playing and the scent of fresh baked rolls or some type of sweet pastry. I looked to the left and saw Shelly sitting on a bar stool facing the counter and Jeff at one next to her facing the door. He locked eyes with me, per usual, and I suddenly felt at ease. Maybe this wouldn't be so bad after all.

I walked across the main entryway and moved into a bar stool next to Jeff.

"Hello you two. I hope I'm not intruding, Shelly. Jeff asked me to join you."

Shelly looked up in disgust, but mustered a smile and nodded, "No worries from me. The more the merrier. So, what's so important that you two needed to bombard me with this awkward encounter? I mean I feel like I've already expressed my feelings clearly to you, Alicia."

Jeff interjected before I could react. "Well, Shelly, Alicia explained to me that you shared with her that we were still married and still living together. She also explained that I had the emotional capacity of a dead person when it comes to intimate relationships, so yeah, I'd say you just about covered all your regular highlights."

Shelly turned a frightening shade of red and I worried she might explode if she didn't speak her mind.

143

"Jeff, I don't understand why you're getting so defensive. I was just trying to keep you two from hurting each other. Alicia deserves to know the truth."

I planned on remaining silent until I was formally invited into the conversation, but I just couldn't hold my breath.

"Okay, both of you, this is getting a little weird for me. Why don't I leave you to it? You can work out all the kinks and then maybe Jeff, you can give me a call later."

Jeff jumped to his feet and grabbed me before I could take off. "Alicia, we're not married. We're not in any type of relationship. Shelly, I've tried to remain friendly with you. I've been kind and patient, but you've taken it too far this time. Mine and Alicia's relationship, if you'd call it that this early, is new and delicate, but it's between us and I'm warning you to butt out."

"You're warning me? I think you better think things through. There's lots of water under the bridge that you could drown in if you're not careful. I know things. Things that would destroy you in this small town you love so much."

"Bring it on Bitch! I'm not worried about your threats. All you've done is ensure that I will have absolutely NOTHING to do with you from now on. We're done talking. Stay away from me and stay away from Alicia! Come on Alicia, we're going."

I was shocked but prepared to let Jeff lead me wherever he saw fit. I had already felt a pull towards submitting to this man. God, help me.

Obviously I hadn't known Jeff that long, but I was amazed by his forcefulness and his language. I know

I should have been turned off by it, but I found his reaction oddly comforting, and honestly, a little bit of a turn on. It was good to know that when necessary, Jeff would jump to my defense and take the proper action.

Jeff grabbed my hand and drug me through the main floor of the restaurant through the front door. He continued to move at hyper speed until we reached about a ½ mile from my apartment. He then stopped in the middle of the sidewalk and turned to face me. "Alicia, I love you. I know it's early and you're probably not where I am and that's okay, but I want you to know how I feel. I'm ready to build something solid; something real. I don't want you to hear this and think I'm expecting something from you. I just want a chance to prove this could be something real, at least for me."

I stood there in silence; paralyzed by his words. I said nothing. I just leaned in and gently kissed him, then turned while still holding his hand and we walked together, still in silence, back to my apartment.

The next morning, I woke to the smell of fresh coffee and what I believed to be cinnamon rolls. It smelled wonderful and I was getting ready to get up and head to the kitchen when Jeff walked through the bedroom door with a pizza pan holding a cup of coffee, with cream and sugar this time, and a plate with quite possibly the largest cinnamon roll I'd ever seen. I smiled and scooted back into my bed. "Where did you get that mammoth cinnamon roll? It looks and smells delicious."

He smiled and said, "I have a few tricks up my sleeve. Scoot over so we can have breakfast in bed."

I sipped the coffee and Jeff fed me a bite of the roll. It was delicious and I thought to myself, I could get use to this kind of attention and pampering. I could tell that he was feeling uncomfortable about my awkward silence about his declaration of love after just a week of dating. I did feel these things for him, but I was afraid. It's exactly what I wanted, but I didn't want it over false pretenses. I didn't want him to project whatever feelings he has had for Shelly onto this new relationship between us. But what if he really did feel these things? What if he really did love me? What do I stand to lose? If I say nothing and he gets discouraged he might retreat. I couldn't bear to lose him. This is the first time in over 20 years that I had felt anything other than sadness, loneliness, and heartache. But my heart and my mind told very different stories. If I took a chance, it could end in heartache as well. What if it fails? But what if it turns out to be the happy ending I've been dreaming of? I decided that anything worth having was worth the risk. So, I cautiously jumped, if that's even a thing.

"Jeff, I love you too. I'm scared and I'm worried we're moving way too fast, but I do feel these things for you, so I'm going to take a chance. I know that you want a simple life, but life isn't simple. I don't want just a simple life. I want to complicate things and see where they lead."

Jeff moved the tray to the floor and rolled over on top of me. He began kissing me, gently, and for hours he just kissed me and touched me; not necessarily sexual, but more intimately. He rubbed my arms and massaged my legs and feet. He carried me into the bathroom and filled my bathtub up with steaming hot water and a lilac bubble bath that he apparently had purchased when he went hunting for the cinnamon rolls. He lit the candle next to my tub and then placed my completely exposed body, physically and emotionally, into the warm bubble bath. He undressed and slid in behind me in the tub. He grabbed a cup and began wetting my hair down. Then he pumped some shampoo into his hand and began massaging it through my hair. I'd never had anyone wash my hair for me or draw me a bubble bath for that matter. The act was sensual and very stimulating. He then grabbed my loofah and lathered it up and washed the parts of my body he could reach without moving from the position behind me. I was so excited I couldn't react appropriately. I wanted him and he knew it.

I stood up once I was rinsed off and grabbed a towel and threw it on the bathroom floor. He stood up from the tub and kneeled to the floor. We made love on the floor of my bathroom. It was sensual and unexpected, and quite possibly the most erotic sexual experience I had ever had. Once finished, I just laid there, drinking him and the glow of our lovemaking in. I loved him and he loved me and that was all that mattered, at least for this moment.

Chapter 15-Love at Face Value

Weeks went by and neither of us had heard from Shelly. It seemed as if the main problem in our relationship had faded away and we were happy and in love. Our relationship had been moving at warp speed and it seemed to be working for us. I gave notice to my New York column and started writing for the advice column in the *Fary Banks Gazette.* It didn't pay much, but the work was fulfilling, and I had plenty of money saved from my divorce with Max. Life seemed almost too good to be true. Jeff had been a little busier than when we first met, flipping several new houses, and I hadn't seen him in several days because of it. He was coming for dinner tonight and I was determined to make him something special; especially since he hadn't seen me cook anything since we met. To be honest, I ordered some upscale take out for our dinner, but I fully intended to place the takeout on my two plastic plates and to snazzy up the table with a couple of candles and a bottle of red. I knew he'd be impressed at just the gesture. I decide to wear some new lingerie instead of putting on a dress for our reunion. It didn't really matter what I wore; it wouldn't stay on me for long anyway.

Around 5:30 Jeff knocked once on the door and then walked in. He had a bouquet of sunflowers in his hands, my favorite, and handed them off to me as he pecked my cheek. It was kind and gentle, but a little disappointing. I guess I was expecting a romantic movie entrance with a long, deep kiss, but the peck on the cheek was nice. I could tell he was starting to get comfortable with me and our relationship, and for that I could overlook the romantic entrance for the peck. He walked past me and grabbed a glass from the cabinet, filled it with water, and then took the flowers back from me and placed them in the glass on the table.

"Dinner smells great. Where'd you order it from?" Jeff giggled as he said it. He then looked at me with an almost frightening look on his face. He looked more nervous than I've ever seen him. I felt worried and anxious. How can a man bring flowers and giggle one minute, and look like the sky is falling in the next breath?

"Alicia, we need to talk."

Still visibly worried, my voice shaky, "Oh my God, Is it serious?"

He quickly reacted, "I think it is."

My heart began racing, and I felt like I could barely breathe.

I thought to myself, this is it. It's over. Maybe the peck on the cheek meant more than he was simply becoming comfortable in this relationship. Maybe it had become too comfortable. And he didn't even react to my new lingerie. We're over for sure! Still, I collected myself.

"What is it Jeff? Just tell me."

Almost hesitantly, Jeff grabbed my hands and placed them in his.

"I just think it's time that we make this situation a little more permanent. I think we should move in together. What do you think? I just want you to be the first and last thing I see every day. I don't like it when three or four days go by, and we barely speak or touch. And I'd really like to see you in this little number more frequently."

Jeff laughed and raised his eyebrows flirtatiously.

"I'd suggest we move in to my place, but as you know, it's just a little studio by the lighthouse. It's not really set up for a couple; it's more of a bachelor pad. It's not even that, honestly; more of a drop in the bed after work hut. It was a perk of my job, and they included it in my retirement since I wasn't married. I live there for free, so I could definitely take care of the rent here for us. I'm sure the new guy would love to take it over. What do you think?"

Relieved I screamed, "Well Shit Jeff. I thought the worst was going to happen!"

Jeff giggled and then straightened his face back up and said, "I was being serious about us, that's all."

"Well, did you tell your face Jeff? You can't use the same expression for every conversation you have with me. I thought you were dying or dumping me. But yes. I think you're right. Let's do it!"

It was finally happening. My happy ending seemed to be within reach. I knew deep down we were moving too quickly. Aside from the color of his eyes and the way his body moved in synch with mine, I really didn't know much about Jeff. What I did know was that life was too short for what ifs, so again, I jumped, secretly praying I wouldn't fall to my death.

We enjoyed our dinner and then he enjoyed dessert. I fell asleep in his arms and woke with a new appreciation for this life we were making. From now on I would fall asleep with the love of my life and wake to see him lying next to me.

To celebrate our decision, we spent the entire day in bed, eating, watching movies, and making love. It was a lazy day. We were taking the next big step in our relationship and to celebrate it, we did absolutely nothing at all, which was perfect.

Chapter 16-Taking Action

Once we were comfortable with our new living arrangements and created a good flow, we both secretly began to wonder when the walls would start crashing down. We still hadn't heard from or so much as caught a glance from Shelly. We were still basking in the newness of our love and things were going great, but the threat of Shelly still cast a dark cloud which was constantly lingering above our relationship and our happiness. And to boot, we still hadn't had a real conversation about Max. I mentioned him in a few passing conversations as my ex, but that was it. I know it seemed deceitful, but I just didn't think we had room for anymore crazy in our developing relationship. And we were happy. So why not stay in the happiness bubble for as long as we possibly could?

We got ready separately this morning, me in the bathroom and Jeff already cleaned up and ready for the day, quietly sitting on the back patio sipping coffee with a biscotti he had picked up from *The Beanery.* I was nibbling on mine in front of the bathroom mirror all while brushing through my hair and applying a little makeup. Once ready, I grabbed my coffee cup from the bath counter and headed out to the patio to sit with my love. The summer moved in quickly and it was humid, with just a touch of a coastal breeze that kissed our faces with a faint dusting of salt from the air. We finished up our coffee and headed out for some shopping.

As we approached the ferry, I just let the breeze hit my face, walking slowly up the ramp trying to take in the moment. We lived in such a lovely place. I had difficulty remembering why I had been so miserable before. Honestly, I've always appreciated the little things; it was the loneliness that had taken me over in the past. And it wasn't beyond my understanding that in one fell swoop my life could change, and the loneliness would set back in. So, I was living in the moment.

Once we made it on deck, Jeff turned to face me and held both of my hands. He continued to stare into my eyes, and I was overcome with joy, deep within. We were halfway across the water when we heard a familiar voice.

"Well if it isn't the lovebirds...how sweet."

We both turned and to our unfortunate surprise, there stood Shelly. She looked frazzled; her hair looked as if it hadn't been brushed in some time and her leisure clothes were barely a step up from pajamas.

Jeff spoke first. " Hi Shelly." He sarcastically continued. " Looks like you're doing well."

"No, I'm not doing well, Jeff. You up and dumped me like yesterday's garbage for your new floozy. "

I started to speak to defend myself from her accusations when Jeff placed one hand in front of my mouth as to hush me.

He looked sternly at her, and approached her, almost in a fit of rage, and said, "Go as far away as possible from us to the opposite end of the ferry. Never approach us again. Consider yourself warned."

Shelly stomped her feet like a small child and leaned in towards Jeff and violently screamed, "Don't threaten me, Jeff. You know what I'm capable of."

Then she smiled at me with a quirky fake smile and said, "Enjoy your day, Alicia. I hear it's going to be lovely. "

Then she turned and walked away.

After the appropriate amount of time, allowing her to make some distance from us, I turned back towards

Jeff. I was beside myself. It was clear to me Shelly
was beyond crazy.

"Jeff, what are we going to do? She's never going to
leave us alone. It's obvious she just put some time
between our last meeting to build up stamina. She's
been plotting since the day she heard my name."

"Alicia, it's nothing to worry about. She's just blowing
off steam. She's jealous. She'll get over it in time.
We'll just continue to avoid her."

I nodded unconvincingly and turned my stare in the
other direction. I was not convinced, and I knew,
deep down, I needed to oversee this myself. In the
darkest part of my mind, I knew if I didn't make this
problem go away, we'd have a fatal attraction, dead
rabbit scenario on our hands. And so, while Jeff
spent his afternoon enjoying the sunshine, the
breeze, and the carefree day we'd planned shopping,
I spent mine plotting a revenge plan in my head.

And what did she mean by, "You know what I am capable of?" I should have pushed, but honestly I was afraid of the response.

The next morning, I decided to go to the shooting range at *Jefferson's Farm*. Most people go there to blow off some steam or to improve their skill, but I had never even shot a gun before, and I had zero skill when it came to shooting. Daddy had bought me a Glock 43 x when I was still living at home. It was pretty, black cherry red with a diamond accent. I always thought it was too pretty to shoot anyway, but now I felt compelled to learn. I wasn't necessarily planning on using it, but for no other reason than protection, I thought it would be a good idea to at least learn how to load and fire off a shot. I chose not to share my plans for the day with Jeff. He was a gun enthusiast, and though this would probably excite him and maybe even bring us closer, my intentions were not completely pure, and so I told my first lie

in our relationship and told him I was going to go do

girl things; hair salon, nail salon and so forth. I

needed to be crafty with my time because though he

might not notice a trim, he'd notice if my nails hadn't

been fixed, so I would have to stop by the nail salon

after the range for a quick appointment. I stopped

out on the patio to give Jeff a kiss and headed off for

some shooting lessons.

I needed to take a cab to *Jefferson's Farm* as it was

out in the country a bit. Before hailing a cab, I

walked over to *The Beanery* to grab my caramel

latte. I figured I would need extra caffeine to get

through this experience. After grabbing my coffee, I

headed towards the farm; about eleven miles away

from town. When I arrived, Jim Johnson met me at

the front and approached with a big smile. He was

an older gentleman, about 65 years old, and he was

wearing old, torn up jean overalls and a dirty, once white, tank top undershirt. He had a hat on with the *Johnson Farm* insignia and he was missing a few of his front teeth. Nice guy, but it made me feel a little unsettled about shooting a gun under his direction. "Good morning, Mr. Johnson, I'm Alicia. We spoke on the phone. I'd like some lessons or at least a little direction with learning to shoot." Mr. Johnson grinned through the teeth he had and replied, "Well Hi there little lady. You can call me Jimmy. I'm happy to help you out. I assume you brought your own gun and ammo."

"Yes sir. They're in my little satchel here." I could see Jimmy eyeing my bright pink, sparkling gun bag and I also knew without a doubt he was making fun of me, but I didn't care. Surely, he's met a real lady before. I refused to be embarrassed of my strong ability to accessorize. It was a necessary skill in every facet of my life, so I just grinned back and followed him, sparkly pink satchel proudly in hand.

"Back this way little lady. To the back half of the property."

Once we made it to the area designated for shooting on the farm, Jimmy led me back to a private stall and asked me to lay my gun and bullets on the board in front of me. He said, "Go ahead and load the gun." I smiled nervously and said, "Well Jimmy, I don't even know how to do that. This is going to be a full lesson if you don't mind."

He snickered again and I felt even more uncomfortable. I was hopeful someone else would show up to help besides Jimmy. "Okay little lady, hand me the gun."

As he picked up my little rose-colored gun, he continued to snicker and shake his head. I was mortified, when in reality, I should have been proud of the beautiful gift my daddy gave me. I just didn't feel the need to share my gun's significance with a stranger, so I continued to listen and tried to ignore what I viewed as disrespect. Mr. Johnson continued with the lesson and I re-focused on his words rather than my feelings.

"So, you push the magazine release like this and then load the bullets. Sometimes it's difficult because of the spring. Then put the magazine back against the well, like this."

He demonstrated each step, and I was mentally taking notes, praying I'd remember all of them.

"Then pull down on the magazine to make sure it's seated properly. You don't want your gun to malfunction. And make certain not to point the gun at anyone or anything unless you plan to shoot right then. Pull the slide back until it stops. When it's back far enough, it will snap forward, like this. It's now ready to go. Are you?" He snickered again and I became increasingly agitated. Maybe I was no longer in the frame of mind to do this today.

I nodded anyway and took hold of the gun, holding it down towards the ground until I was given the next step. Mr. Johnson came up behind me and placed his hands on my right hand to demonstrate the proper holding and stance. Then he yelled, "Fire."

I stood there frozen. "Shoot the gun towards the big target in the field, Alicia. You won't hurt anything."

I stood there again, afraid to move. He gave me a few minutes before saying anything else.

"Alicia, double click the trigger with your finger and fire." His voice was calmer and almost comforting. He could tell how nervous I was. So, I let him guide my hand as I prepared to shoot the gun. It didn't hit the center of the target, but it did hit the paper on the side, and I felt it to be exhilarating. I paused and smiled at Mr. Johnson. "There ya go little lady. Do it again." And so, I shot round after round at the target. Once out of bullets, I reloaded on my own and shot again. After an hour or so, I was getting much closer to the center of the target. Not a professional by any means, but I felt much more comfortable with my decision. Once we were finished, he went through the process of properly cleaning and putting my gun away. I felt accomplished and happy with my progress.

"Thank you, Mr. Johnson. I'd like to come back once or twice a week if that's okay to continue practicing."

"I reckon that would be okay. Wednesdays and Fridays work in your schedule, around the same time?"

"Yes, sir. I'll be here. What do I owe for today?"

"Nothing for today. It was enjoyable to watch. We'll talk turkey at your next lesson."

I smiled and thanked him again and called for a taxi to get back to the nail salon before Jeff grew suspicious.

Once I made it back to town, I stopped in and had a pedicure instead. I could show off my toes and that would keep Jeff from being suspicious. I took my fancy gun purse into the bedroom and hid it in my dresser. He wouldn't be suspicious of the gun bag, because after all, it just looked like a purse. I walked through the small apartment calling his name but couldn't find him anywhere. I grabbed my cell phone and gave him a ring, but it went straight to voicemail. It was around two in the afternoon, and it felt odd that he had left and didn't call, text, or even leave a note. I was exhausted and just didn't have the energy to go hunt him down, so I undressed, cracked my window, and got into bed to take a little nap. I needed some rest. The lessons were more stressful than I had expected, and keeping secrets from Jeff was even more draining.

Chapter 17-People Change: Seasons Change

I slept through the night, from late afternoon when I decided to take a quick nap, until the birds started chirping out my window at five a.m. I don't think I have ever slept that long before, so I apparently needed the rest. I rolled over to see Jeff asleep beside me; I didn't even hear him come in and I still was uncertain of where he had been. I rolled over to check my phone; no texts or missed phone calls, so obviously he just came back home and noticed me sleeping and left me alone.

I decided to throw on some clothes and walk down to *The Beanery* to grab a cappuccino and some pastries for breakfast. It was warm, muggy, and my hair was sticking to my face even as early in the morning as it was. I grabbed a clip from my purse and pulled my hair back. I was excited to walk in the coffee shop with the air conditioning blowing full force. After ordering, I took a seat at my table. It had been a month of Tuesdays since I had sat there. Literally. I thought how curious it was that life could change so dramatically in such a short period of time. The barista called my name, I gathered my food and coffees and headed back to see Jeff, still curious as to where he had been and why he hadn't checked in with me yesterday. I walked into the apartment to find Jeff already sitting on the patio. I walked out, breakfast and coffee in hand, and decided to just smile and pretend the awkwardness wasn't covering us.

"Good morning. I've got breakfast."

Jeff turned and smiled and reached up for a kiss. "Thanks Darlin. How was your sleep?"

Great, I thought to myself. I'm not going to be able to lie. He is going to know I'm pissy about his secretive rendezvous yesterday. My face never lies; offers no deliverance whatsoever.

"Well, it was premature. You weren't here when I returned from my errands, and I tried to call you with no answer. I decided to take a nap because honestly, I was exhausted and really had nothing else to do but worry. I woke to you beside me, but no texts or calls from you. I apparently needed the rest because I slept for about 16 hours. So, the real question is, where were you that was so important you couldn't leave a note or send a text, or make a quick call?"

I could feel my face heating up and I wasn't certain if my appearance was giving off the right vibe. Sometimes irritated and embarrassed looked the same on me, and to be honest, I wasn't sure I wanted to show the flustered side of me to Jeff this early on. I mean, I guess I should be willing to give him the benefit of the doubt. It's just that my history hasn't been wonderful when it comes to trusting the men that I love to do what's right; and I guess if I had shared this tidbit with Jeff, he might have been a little more forthcoming. So, it's partially my fault, but still, he could send a text for crying out loud.

Jeff snickered and smiled back at me, and it simply infuriated me.

Now I was certain my flushed face showed anger and irritation.

"Jeff, whatever it is or was, I don't think it's funny at all."

"Alicia, Darlin, you're making a big deal out of nothing, I promise."

"Men. Grr."

My mind was like a whirlwind of crazy. I thought to myself, it's just like a man to desensitize everything and take whatever hurt they've inflicted on us and turn it back on the woman. I wouldn't be acting crazy if he didn't do something to make me feel that way. It's an uneven web of emotions in a relationship. The woman feels everything, and the man feels whatever he chooses. I wasn't sure at this point if I wanted to slap him or cry. So, I just took a seat and said nothing. He was still grinning and snickering a little under his breath which was infuriating.

The silent treatment was the easiest way to prevent me from doing and saying things I might regret later, and quite frankly, the most effective way to get back at a man in my experience. So instead of entertaining whatever he had to say, I began to nibble on my croissant after tossing his on the table in front of him. Sip, nibble, sip, nibble. I'll just enjoy the morning and try to put his bullshit out of my mind for a while.

After we both ate and sipped in silence, him still with a shitty grin on his face, he turned to me hesitantly, as if he had something important to say but was uncertain. I'm sure at this point he was probably afraid of me. After all, he hasn't had the best track record with sane and honest relationships either, so I tried to fake a small smile to put him at ease. Why, I'm uncertain. The psychology behind why women try to inadvertently comfort men even when they've done something to hurt them is beyond the scope of my expertise. It's odd, but seems to come naturally; a maternal instinct, I guess.

"Well, Alicia, I was going to wait for this; something a little better planned out, but I suppose now is as good of time as any. Just so you know, this is what I was working on yesterday, and I wanted it to be a surprise, but I can tell that if I wait to explain myself much longer, things are going to get heated and even more awkward here, so, here it goes."

Jeff reached into his pocket and pulled out a little red velvet box. It wasn't blue or black, traditional for rings, so I was still overly curious as to what was taking place. He then stood in front of me and proceeded to kneel on to one knee.

Suddenly, I couldn't breathe. I could feel my face getting redder and redder; probably covered in hives at this point from the humidity, the stress of not knowing what has been taking place these past 24 hours, and now the anxiety of what appeared to be a proposal. A very quick one, I might add, for only dating a few short months.

"Alicia, I love you. I wasn't sure I'd ever be ready to fully commit to someone again until I saw your face at the coffee shop so many months ago. Now, I can't imagine my life without you. It wasn't love at first sight for you, I'm certain, but for me it was so much deeper than that. I spent years gathering up the tattered remnants of my dignity after heartache, and then you came into my life and healed me. With you, I feel complete. I know how cliché that sounds, but it's true. We're not getting any younger and life's too short to spend any time with regrets. Sometimes when you know, you know. I'm sorry this seemed so deceitful, but I really wanted it to be a surprise. And as a bonus, I now know how you'll react if I do upset you." Jeff tried his hardest not to giggle.

"Darlin, would you do me the honor of being my wife?"

I sat there staring deeply into his green eyes as tears filled mine. I wanted to jump up at once and toss my arms around him and scream yes, but I froze for a few moments. He saw me so clearly that he could almost see through me. The connection was so very strong, but it worried me, and it was evident on my face. I began to fear that he was changing his mind. He could tell I was uncertain about something, and Jeff doesn't do uncertain. It was now or never, that was obvious.

"Yes, Jeff, I will marry you. I cannot think of anything that would mean more to me than being your wife. I love you. But what the hell is wrong with you? Every time you have an idea for something special, especially when it comes to our relationship, you come at me backwards with all of this secretive shit. I have trust issues. Maybe I haven't been clear about that, but I'm making you aware now. You are the love of my life, but please know, I need clarity. I worry too much. You had me scared to death that something bad was happening. That's three times you've done this. You've got to work on your game face. Seriously."

I stood up and kissed him, passionately, and he picked me up and carried me through the threshold of our patio door and back into our bedroom. We made love, and it felt different, in a good way. I rolled over afterwards, fully satisfied, and then the negative thoughts reentered my head. I wanted him so badly I almost ruined it. I am an overthinker. I just needed a little light after the darkness, and he put light back in my life. I should have told him how I was feeling in that very moment as we can never have that moment in time back...quite possibly one of the most important moments of my life, but I just couldn't form the words, so I basically yelled at him while accepting his marriage proposal. And in the past, that wouldn't have helped me anyway. Max would not have cared how I was feeling, and I still felt the threat of rejection for my thoughts and feelings deep in my soul.

I rolled out of bed and went to the kitchen to get some juice. Jeff was back asleep after what I assume was a stressful exchange with me, followed by joy, followed by strenuous love making. I'm sure he was exhausted, and I just needed a break from the chaos stirring inside of my mind.

After his mid-afternoon nap, I asked him what his plans were. I guess I just wanted a timeline of how soon he wanted to get married and officially start our life together.

"Do you feel rested, love? I figured you needed a little nap after everything?"

"Yes, Darlin, thank you. I've been busy planning all of this for a while. I know it doesn't sound romantic, but I planned on popping the question at *The Beanery,* since that's where it all started, but after running around yesterday and finalizing everything, I realized that I hadn't left you a note. I didn't want to lie to you, but I also didn't want you to feel suspicious, and a text would have led to a lie of some sort, so I just decided to let it go and deal with the consequences today...ha ha, but then you were so visibly upset, I just decided here and now was as good of a time as any. So anyway, I'm thinking of an Autumn wedding, maybe September 15th. It falls on a Saturday and it will still be mild weather here. Maybe on the beach with just us and a couple others to witness. What do you think?"

I couldn't help but smile. I was super excited that we would only have to wait three short months to be husband and wife. Funny how three short months sounds different when you're planning something exciting, unlike me thinking to myself, we haven't even been dating three months, but I'm happy, so who cares about that little detail anyway?

"That sounds wonderful. I am so excited! I hate to bring this up at such a happy time, but do you think Shelly is going to be a problem?"

"I hope not, but after the fit she threw on the ferry, I'm a little concerned that she might make a scene if she finds out the specific details. So, I think it's best if we just keep it to ourselves. You know, keep our life private. It's not anyone else's business anyway what we do with our lives."

"Okay. I get it, and you're probably right. So, an Autumn wedding on the beach, just you and me. Sounds perfect."

Chapter 18-Preparations

Once Jeff and I decided on a date, I knew the next few months would be a whirlwind of excitement, stress, and emotion. I still wanted to sneak off to my weekly shooting lessons, because quite honestly, I still didn't feel safe. Obviously, I didn't plan on shooting anyone, but Shelly was crazy, and I wouldn't put it past her to put us in danger at some point. Plus, my future husband enjoyed shooting and guns in general, and I thought it would be nice for me to share in some of his interests. I continued to go twice a week and let Mr. Johnson show me a few things. I was getting pretty good too; I was finally able to hit the center of the target about 50% of the time, so that was great progress after just a few weeks. Mr. Johnson said that he had misjudged me; that I was a natural. I did hate misleading Jeff, as I had to make up some random errand every time I went; luckily most of the appointments coincided with his work on flipping houses so most days he didn't even know I was gone. My plan was to just tell him I was learning to shoot as a surprise for him; a way for us to connect with a mutual hobby. Hopefully, his reaction would be like mine when I realized about his secret engagement planning.

June passed quickly for us, and we were stuck right in the hottest month of the year in Maine. July 4th was this coming weekend and Fary Banks always had the best street fair and fireworks. Jeff was excited about the events, but I was hesitant. Anything that pulled a bunch of people in this town together would surely drag out Shelly, and I didn't want to deal with her shit this weekend or ever for that matter.

The eve before the 4th approached, and for the first time, I had someone to sit on the patio and celebrate with. I couldn't help but think of how badly I had wanted to entertain on my patio, which then led me to wonder, where are all of Jeff's friends? In all the months we had been together, he had not introduced me to one other person, aside from the nut job, Shelly, and until this very moment, I thought nothing about it. Maybe the town celebrations this week would uncover a few of his friends, I quietly thought to myself. Hopefully anyway. It was so odd to me that this hadn't crossed my mind before. I felt a wave of concern come over me, hyper focused on whether Jeff had more to hide than just crazy old Shelly.

Why am I like this? Instead of spending the rest of the evening dwelling on this, I just decided to face the concern, discreetly. I'd just strike up a conversation about friends and see how it developed. I didn't want to scare off the one good thing that had happened to me in 20 some years, but my curiosity was killing me.

"So, Jeff, how are you feeling about the weekend? Are you excited about the street fair? I've never been to it, but it has always looked like a good time from my window."

Maybe he'd give me a little more insight before tomorrow, though I didn't plan on pushing him unless I had to.

After a few minutes, Jeff looked up from the paper and smiled with that half wink. He knew a smile and a wink would put my mind at ease, regardless of the situation.

"Well Darlin, this is my 53rd Independence Day in this town. I'm sure it will be a great party, but this stuff doesn't really excite me like it used to. It's my first one with you, so I'm sure it will be memorable."

Memorable, I thought to myself. I hope he means in a good way.

I hopped back into the conversation in hopes he'd offer up a little more information.

"Well, I'm excited. I haven't really participated in anything since I've lived here. Usually just order a pizza and drink a bottle of red on the patio watching the fireworks by myself. Who do you usually watch the fireworks with?"

I was hoping this would drag something out of him.

"I used to watch them with Shelly. The past few years I've just watched them from afar and didn't really join in the local festivities. For several years I have went with Hank and Joe, my two friends that help me fix up houses to flip."

Hmm. So, there's two friends, I thought to myself.

"So, this Hank and Joe, when will I meet them? Do they have wives or girlfriends? Would be nice to finally have that get together on this patio."

"Honestly, Darlin, it's been a whirlwind of events since we met and we've both been so busy, I just haven't had a chance. Of course, I want you to meet them. Hank has a girlfriend, Melinda. They are basically married. They've both just had so many failed relationships in their past that they decided marriage wasn't for them. Joe has been married to Marie for 20 years. You'd like these ladies. I'm sorry, I haven't intentionally procrastinated on introducing you to the gals. I'll call the guys and see if they want to meet up with us downtown tomorrow. How would you feel about them coming over for wine and pizza on the patio and we can watch the fireworks here?"

"That sounds wonderful, Jeff. I've wanted to have people over ever since I moved into this apartment. Let me know once you've talked to them. This is so exciting!"

Jeff grabbed his phone and made a few calls. I went into the kitchen to make a couple sandwiches for us, mainly because I didn't want to seem like I was listening in on his conversations. When I came back with the sandwiches he smiled and said they were looking forward to meeting me and they'd meet us around ten in the morning here at our apartment, and after a little visiting, we'd head to the street fair together. I was overjoyed about the opportunity to make a couple friends. I was kind of concerned still that after all this time I had to ask about friends instead of him willingly introducing me without a push. Regardless, I was determined to make a good impression.

"Okay Jeff, I'm going to walk to the grocery and the liquor store to get some supplies for tomorrow night."

"Hold on a minute and I'll throw on some shorts and go with you. Let's make this a memory of us doing it together."

I felt instantly relieved. I didn't want to beg him to go places with me, and I didn't want to seem needy, but I loved that he usually volunteered to go with me. It brought me such joy that he always chose me over everything else and I was only praying that this would continue as our relationship grew.

So, Jeff and I headed to the store and grabbed some tortilla chips, salsa, and some nuts. We also grabbed 4 bottles of red wine, a 12 pack of light beer, some margarita mix, pineapple juice for a mixer, and an apple pie that looked decent for store-bought. We then stopped at the liquor store and grabbed a bottle of light rum and tequila. We'd already had sandwiches for lunch, but still decided to stop by the bar and have an appetizer and a beer. I wasn't a big fan of beer, but Jeff was, so I was trying different IPA's and drafts to have another thing in common with him. The sour peach draft was pretty good. He even made fun of that choice, saying it wasn't really a beer if it had a sweet or sour aftertaste, but at least I was trying. The place was packed for early Friday afternoon; apparently everyone was already off work for the holiday weekend. Jeff sipped and snacked and smiled at me. Everything seemed right with the world until the tornado, which was better known as Shelly, swept through the bar.

I heard a shrill voice from behind my barstool. Shelly, of course.

"Well, if it isn't the love birds again, doing absolutely nothing on a Friday afternoon."

She walked up and touched my shoulder. My first instinct was to flip around and slap her, but I remained calm for Jeff's sake.

"Well, Shelly, what a pleasure it is to see you here today. You're looking well," I said sarcastically while half rolling my eyes. Jeff just sat there and acted as if he hadn't heard her or even seen her walk in.

"Jeff, aren't you going to say Hello to me?"

"Hey."

"Well, that was warming."

"Shelly, we don't want to see you! We don't want to talk to you! We don't want anything to do with you at all," Jeff said with a raised voice.

I wasn't comfortable with his tone; I've never heard him raise his voice before, not even on the ferry.

"Well, it's a free country, Jeff. I can be wherever I want to be. You two don't own the town."

Shelly leaned in between us, and I was becoming increasingly agitated. Then she gasped as if something had struck her right in the chest.

"What the hell is on her finger? You've got to be kidding me! You barely even know each other. Are you that desperate for attention? Both of you? I just can't believe that you would fall for her bullshit, Jeff. You have no idea what you're doing."

That was it, I was going to punch the bitch. Right here. Right now. I stood up and looked down at her, raised my fist, and popped her right in the left cheek. Jeff gasped and stood up, jumping behind Shelly as if he was preparing to catch her if she fell. She didn't fall, but merely grabbed her left cheek and looked at me in awe.

Jeff screamed, "Alicia, what the hell are you doing?"

"Seriously, Jeff, you're going to defend this bitch over me?"

"Alicia, I'm not defending her. She's psycho, but you just stood up and punched her in a bar in broad daylight like it was nothing."

"I'm tired of her intrusions. I'm tired of her nasty comments towards me. And right now, I'm tired of you defending her. Get her some ice. Nurse her back to health. Whatever! I'm going home."

Before either of them could say or do anything, I had the bags in my hand and rushed out of the bar. I was fuming mad, and I didn't want to hear anything from anyone.

As I marched back to the house, half stomping and half sprinting, I realized how much shit we had bought that I was now carrying by myself for a two-mile trip on foot. I knew that I shouldn't have hit her, but seriously, how much more can I take? And I understand his shock, but his allegiance should be to me; not the crazy person who stalks us and threatens our happiness. I was going to have to think long and hard before I continued down this path. Everything I have ever wanted was coming full circle; a fiancé, potential new girlfriends, and a life I didn't have to escape from, and then boom...Shelly. She was determined to ruin everything, and I wasn't even certain Jeff would want me anyway after he witnessed what I was capable of when provoked.

I finally made it home and I placed all the bags on the island. I looked at my right hand and it was black and blue and quite swollen. The adrenaline must have taken over because I wasn't feeling any pain until this very moment. What if I have broken my hand? That would make my writing career interesting for sure. I grabbed a bag of frozen corn out of the freezer and placed it on my hand. Then I snagged a cold bottle of red from my wine cooler and miraculously uncorked it with my left hand. I didn't even grab a glass. This was a drink it straight from the bottle kind of occasion. I was halfway through the bottle when Jeff busted through the door.

"Why did you take off like that with an injured hand and all these bags? I wasn't mad at you. I was shocked. Completely and utterly flabbergasted that you were capable of such a thing; not that it wasn't warranted. I thought Shelly was going to fall backwards and I really didn't want to deal with the legal consequences of that. Who knows? The nut may still press charges against you. And look at your hand. I grabbed an ace bandage on the way back and some aspirin for the pain. Come sit down over here so I can wrap it for you."

I wanted to yell, I really did, but I couldn't. I would have been shocked too, and who knows how I would have reacted if Jeff had jumped up and sucker punched Max.

Jeff shrugged his shoulders while shaking his head as he walked out of the kitchen. He was sending me mixed signals and I wasn't sure what to do with it all. I decided just to stay quiet and let him take care of me and then we could deal with everything later that evening. I was a tad bit concerned that the dumbass, Shelly, might press charges, and then what? I just sat and continued to drink my wine. Jeff returned to the kitchen and gently lifted the bag of corn off my hand. He sat it aside and began wrapping it. He then tossed two aspirins in my mouth which I reluctantly swallowed with wine. He sat down, took the wine from my left hand, and took a big swig himself.

"We've got to figure this all out, Alicia. We can't live like this. If we must, we will get a restraining order, but I doubt that will stop her. And we will need to wait and see if she files charges against you for punching her today. I'm certain it's going to leave a mark. How is your hand feeling? Should we go to the hospital?"

"No, I'll be fine. Let's get this stuff put away and pretend this didn't happen and not spend any time worrying about it until we need to. I won't punch her again. You have my word on that."

We spent the evening on the patio sipping wine, which neither of us needed at this point, quietly watching the sunset, with very little conversation between us. We decided to call it an early night and we went to bed. Neither of us were in the mood to do anything at all. The next morning, I woke to the sound of someone pounding on my door. My first thought was that Shelly had called the police and they were here bright and early to arrest me, but I was mistaken. Instead of the law, it was Shelly. I thought to myself, I think I would prefer to be arrested.

I walked up to the door, and she began pounding harder. I opened the door, just a crack.

"Shelly, what in the hell are you doing here? What do you want?" I took a minute to notice the small bruise above her left cheek from the altercation at the bar. I felt relieved, even amid her pounding, that she didn't appear to be hurt significantly.

"Let me in you stupid Bitch! You can't just move in on someone else's husband and expect them to just sit back and smile. I'm fighting for what is mine. Now let me in dammit!"

"Jeff...get up and get in here. This crazy bitch is trying to break in the house. I can't hold her back."

Jeff ran through the apartment in his boxer shorts, and I, for some reason, was able to pause in my hatred for this woman to notice how hot he looked. What in the Hell is wrong with me? He busted through the front door and came face to face with Shelly, not an inch between them.

"Shelly, I'm warning you. Stop this bullshit! We are not married. We have not been married for a long, long time. I owe you nothing! Alicia owes you nothing! Leave us ALONE!"

I'd rarely heard Jeff raise his voice, and it was always in reaction to Shelly. I was a little frightened and unusually turned on at the same time. The mix of my emotions and reactions confused me, but in this moment, I knew for certain that I was 100% with the right person. Shelly stood in front of my door and just cried; sobbed and said nothing, which was almost more concerning than her yelling and pounding. When she finally spoke again, I almost felt sorry for her. The heartache I experienced with Max and his lies and infidelity came rushing back. I wanted to hug her instead of hating her. Before I could react, she started speaking through her sobs.

"I'm sorry. I really am. I just can't understand why he would leave me for you."

Jeff started screaming again. "Shelly, I did not leave you for Alicia."

I moved in between them. "Jeff, calm down. She is obviously in no shape for anyone, especially you, to be screaming at her."

Jeff grabbed my arm and pulled me aside out of Shelly's ear reach. He said quietly and calmly, "Alicia, I'm not attacking anyone. She needs to accept the reality of this situation; to finally leave me alone. She needs to leave both of us alone and move on."

"I agree, but I think we need to finesse this a little bit." I stepped back towards Shelly, and I reached my hand out to touch her arm.

She flinched her body back to avoid my touch. I moved closer and wrapped my arms around her. It was a loose hug, not really all that sympathetic feeling, but I knew, as a woman, that she needed to be touched by somebody, even if it was just me.

"Shelly, listen. I know you're hurting. I understand your pain, but your relationship with Jeff has been over for a very long time. I am not what broke the two of you up. I wasn't even a factor at all. I know it's hard to let go of someone you love, but you need to face reality. Jeff and I are going to get married, and you'll just have to accept it. I'd much rather have your blessing than fight every time we see each other, but that will be up to you."

Shelly embraced the hug for a second, sniffed, and stepped back a little.

"I'm sorry. I was able to accept Jeff leaving after a while. I was okay with his flings or whatever you call them after we separated, but this is serious, and I just can't accept it. I always thought he would see what was out there, get bored, and come back to me. I even knew about Jessica, though he said it wasn't that serious. They lasted for several years in between us, but Jeff still maintained his friendship with me and showed up whenever I needed him, so I didn't worry. His work kept him occupied most of the time. You and Jeff, that's different."

Jeff's expression changed. He almost had a sad look in his eyes. Those piercing green eyes had sadness welled up in them, and I didn't like it at all. I couldn't decide if he was in fact feeling something deeper for her or if it was pity, but for some odd reason his ability to empathize with her was comforting to me. He reached out and touched her hand, unbothered by the comments about Jessica, but my mind was racing. Who the hell is Jessica? Maybe this is a conversation for another day, but wow! That means there's more than one crazy bitch to deal with. I tried to re-focus on the task at hand, but this was a lot for one week.

While still touching her hand, Jeff began an attempt at reasoning with her.

"Shelly, I'm sorry you're hurting, and maybe someday we can all be friends, once the newness of this wears off, but for now, Alicia and I need our privacy. As Alicia said, I hope you can find a way to understand and respect our wishes."

Shelly nodded through weepy eyes and whispered once again how sorry she was, then turned and slowly walked away. I decided not to bring up Jessica. He would elaborate when he was ready. Clearly she was a non-issue, or he would have already discussed her with me. And again, I hadn't been completely transparent about Max, so I decided that maybe some things weren't meant to be discussed to death.

Once she was gone, I turned to Jeff and wrapped my arms around him as tight as I could.

"I love you, Jeff. I am sorry she is taking this so hard, and I am sorry you must deal with it. I mean, I guess that we must deal with this, but I love you and I appreciate you so much."

I then kissed him gently and he said not a word. He didn't need to. I knew how he felt and that was enough at this moment.

Chapter 19- Independence

The 4th of July was a celebration from the moment the sun came up. You could hear people in the streets from the front window. The street fair had begun at dawn and people were drinking and eating from the variety of food carts lining Main Street. Laughter filled the air, and I wondered how I had managed to miss out on all the excitement each year since moving here. Jeff's friends would be here by 10:00 a.m. and I wanted to look nice; I desperately wanted to make a good impression. This would be my first real opportunity to have a couple of actual girlfriends. I started to undress to hop in the shower, but Jeff had other plans.

"Come here Darlin. We have plenty of time to get ready. Bring your sweet little self over here and get back into this bed with me."

Somehow, he still had the power to make me blush. It hadn't been a long relationship, but we had spent a lot of time together, so I had expected the butterflies to settle a little by now, but no...not yet. A little embarrassed for some odd reason, I shyly undressed and walked back over to the bed and slid back in beside him.

"What do you have in mind, my love?"

"I don't think words are necessary right now." Again, I was lost in those green eyes. I'm fairly certain he could tell me to do just about anything and those eyes would deliver the intended result. Those damn eyes. They'll surely be the death of me.

He rolled over on top of me, and I was once again focused on his broad chest. His chest was the only other feature that fully competed with his eyes. He was truly perfect, at least for me. I found him so very sexy. He was strong and confident and very capable and willing to meet all my needs and then some. He was your typical 50 something, middle-aged man, but he still had desire and stamina and that was more attractive to me than the act itself. He took his time. He always did. It wasn't a race for him.

He started with my legs and kissed my inner thighs. He moved up and down all the hot spots on my body and landed on my lips. It was so erotic that I often wondered how the act of actual sex itself was necessary. For me, the foreplay was where it was at, and he was always generous in this department. When we finally finished, my mind automatically went to the time, and I suddenly panicked about being ready when his friends arrived. I felt guilty sliding out of the comfort of his arms; the little nook under his arm that allowed me to peacefully rest on his chest. I gave a little tug to his beard, something that likewise turned me on, and I leaned up to kiss his mouth gently one last time, and then jumped to my feet.

"Sorry buddy, I've got to get this party started. Meet me in the shower if you'd like."

He jumped to attention and followed me through the bedroom into the bathroom. I ran like I was literally being chased, giggling as he pinched at my ass. We hopped in the shower, which also took a little bit longer than I had planned, and then we hustled to get dressed. I grabbed out this sparkly, red, white, and blue tank top that I had bought special for today. If I'm being honest, it was probably a bit too youthful for me, but I was excited about celebrating and I knew Jeff would like it, so I bought it anyway. I threw on my cutoff jeans shorts and fixed my hair and makeup and then met Jeff in the kitchen to throw some charcuterie boards together and to chill some wine glasses. I might have been just a touch more excited than I should have been, but Jeff had a way of putting my mind at ease so I felt confident that everything would go smoothly.

About 20 minutes later, Joe and Marie arrived. I welcomed them in and offered Marie a glass of red. We sat and listened to the guys ramble on about cars and the weather. I was noticeably uncomfortable, but I did my best to initiate some conversation with them both. Hank and Melinda arrived a little before 10:30. As we were sipping wine I wished I'd thought of making mimosas instead. I'd always wanted to have brunch with mimosas with close friends. Lost in my own thoughts again I wondered if maybe these new friendships would flourish, and the brunch opportunity would present itself again sometime soon. My trailing thoughts discouraged my focus from the ongoing conversation, so I tried desperately to get my ADHD under control and to refocus on the visit at hand. I made a point of not interrupting conversations and I worked strongly on making eye contact, both of which were huge obstacles for me and often ruined friendships before they began. Melinda and Marie obviously knew each other well and I started to feel a little left out. Melinda seemed to notice my discomfort and decided to direct her glance in my direction, then turned the conversation to include me.

"So, Alicia, I hear you're from Jersey and you have spent quite a bit of time in the big city? A writer or something?"

"Yes. That's right, but I quit my column job a few months ago and started writing locally. I wanted my writing to be a little more authentic and I wanted to focus more time on me and Jeff."

"Very cool," Melinda replied, and Marie nodded with a smile. Then Marie chimed in, "So you're a writer and have been single for some time until Jeff? Sometimes I think we'd all be better off being single. Look what men do to you. Just look at Shelly. She's gone completely mad after Jeff. And I'm pretty sure she played a role in Jessica leaving."

There's that name again. I tried to act as if I was privy to the details of Jeff and Jessica. I forgot momentarily that these ladies knew Jeff when he was with Shelly, and a piece of me was thankful that they at least acknowledged she was a bit crazy, even if it was in sympathy. But I was also a little distracted by the inquisition. Why the big assumption that I have been single for such a long time? Why did they assume Jeff had to rescue me? I mean he did, but they didn't know that. I smiled and explained it a bit more, almost in hopes that they would feel sorry for me too and decide to be my friend, even if not sincerely.

"I was married for a long time to a man named Max. We were very much in love, until we weren't. Max had a lot of extracurricular activities that didn't include me, if you know what I mean. I finally got tired of the narcissistic bullshit and cut my losses and left Jersey. I spent several years living in the city, but I felt so isolated, which is odd for living in a place where millions of people live and visit. I finally realized it just wasn't for me. So, I picked a spot on the map and landed here.

Then I spent years here with no one; no friends, no boyfriend, nothing. Much of that I am learning was my fault; I was just afraid to branch out. Worried about rejection, I guess. So, I understand the better off part, but I am beyond grateful to have found Jeff and I was probably a little too excited to meet you ladies." I felt embarrassed after I said it, but they smiled at me, and the gesture didn't feel like sympathy, so I just sipped and smiled, sipped, and smiled.

Jeff, on the other hand, looked a bit distracted. We hadn't spoke of Max and Jeff had clearly overheard our conversation. But seriously, with this Jessica thing, he had no room to judge. He knew that I was divorced, but none of the sordid details. I smiled and nodded reassuringly at Jeff, and he smirked back as if to say, no biggie. We can talk later.

The day went on as planned and we all seemed to be having a good time. We went down to the street fair around 4 p.m. and had cheese steaks and elephant ears from the food carts. I felt like a kid again. Jeff noticed a drop of icing on my lip and leaned over to lick it off. Marie and Melinda noticed and giggled a bit. I knew they weren't making fun of me, but I also didn't want them to think we were trying to oversell our relationship. My guess was that their relationships were older and getting a little stale, and Jeff's enthusiasm with me created a little spark of envy. In my experience, that usually helped relationships rather than hurting them. If Jeff and I were all lovey dovey, maybe the other two men would take a hint and follow suit. The thing was, we were not acting. We were so in love it scared me. I sat in anticipation, wondering when and if the shoe would drop, and I had already learned with past lovers how anticipation can kill a relationship. We continued to walk the fair and stopped at several booths. We came upon cotton candy, which is one of my very favorite things, though I had never told Jeff that. He turned and smiled and said, "I'll grab us some cotton candy. I know we've already had a bunch of sugar, but I love me some cotton candy, so why not splurge?" I smiled and laughed in agreement. Why am I so giddy over cotton candy?

Why am I so giddy over a grown ass man? I just couldn't help myself. He grabbed some on a stick and we took turns taking bites. Melinda and Marie were most definitely giving their men death glares. I decided maybe we should cool it on the PDA. I whispered my observations to Jeff, and he said, "That's on them. I'm not holding back on account of anyone." He then dipped me back and kissed me right in the middle of the fair in front of everyone. I felt like I was on a movie set, and he was right. Screw it! We're going to stay on this ride for as long as we can.

As the sun started to set, I walked back with the girls and suggested we head to my apartment to sit on the patio and prepare for the fireworks. Marie said that if we had alcohol, she'd follow us anywhere. I smiled and reassured her we had plenty to go around as we headed back. Once we were there, we all grabbed a beer and some of the snacks we had on the counter and headed towards the patio. I grabbed a few blankets just in case anyone felt a bit chilly, and we all sat and talked and laughed and drank like we'd all been friends forever. I guess that was true for the five of them, but it was a new feeling for me, and I loved that I finally had some sense of comradery. The fireworks started just after 9:30 p.m. and the town spared no expense. It was spectacular. I didn't remember it being such a display these past few years, but I had always watched them alone and without any enthusiasm. We ended the night with a few shots and a toast to our upcoming nuptials. It was the first time my house felt like a home, and I was ecstatic.

Chapter 20-Rolling With the Punches

As August approached, Jeff and I both felt comfortable that Shelly had accepted that our relationship couldn't be torn apart, and we believed that the worst with her was behind us. Daddy had been gone for years and I really didn't have a relationship with my mom, so wedding preparations were not that big of a struggle. I was optimistic that Marie and Melinda would show up to the wedding and at least pretend we were friends so that I could feel a sense of acceptance at my own wedding. They had stopped over a few times after the 4th to chat and we did have a few coffee dates, so I was hopeful that some real friendships were starting to bloom. Our wedding was just a little over seven weeks away, and everything was close to perfect. Jeff and I were focused on creating a life we didn't have to escape from, and so far, we had been successful. Our mornings were typically filled with love making, coffee on the patio, or snuggled up in a blanket in the bay window and sharing breakfast together over a shared newspaper. Our afternoons were open to exploring whatever we desired except for the couple of afternoons a week that Jeff worked on home makeovers and making deals with banks to flip houses in the town that needed some extra love. I used those afternoons to go the farm and practice shooting, a small detail I still hadn't shared with Jeff. Our evenings were takeout on the patio or a casual dinner out, always within walking distance so we could walk on the beach afterwards. At night I would nestle into the nook between his arm and chest, and we would watch old black and white movies; movies that told pure love stories before society and Hollywood ruined the perception of love and romance. We were perfect and I couldn't wait to finalize our commitment and marry the love of my life, the man of my dreams. I was still guarded, just a little bit, often wondering if this love bubble would burst uncontrollably without warning, but for the first time in my life, I decided to put my focus on the happy for as long as it lasted and pray that whatever we had would be strong enough to withstand whatever storm might face us in the future. If it did blow up in a cloud of smoke, at least I'd have the memories of a brief, but perfect love story, and that was worth the possibility of heartache and most definitely something worth remembering.

Today started the same as every other day of our lives: Love making, coffee, a pastry over the daily newspaper. After the last bite of his pastry, Jeff looked up and said, "I'm going to head out for a while and talk to Mr. Minter at the bank. I heard there was a new repo down on the west side and I want to get the ball rolling before someone else gets wind of it. Do you have anything planned for the day?"

"I do. Melinda and Marie just sent me a group text asking if I was free for coffee and lunch so I'll just let them know I can make it and we can meet back here before dinner. Eat in or out tonight?

"Let's eat in tonight. After running around all day, I'm sure I'll be ready just to relax at home, if that's okay with you, Darlin?"

"Of course. I'll just pick up some Thai food from the new café downtown and bring it back for us, say around 5?"

"Perfect. Give me a kiss."

I leaned over the counter and kissed him. He tasted like caramel and cocoa beans and his beard smelled of cedar wood and tea tree oil. Everything about this beautiful, green-eyed man was delicious. "I'll miss you. Enjoy your day."

"Ditto, Darlin. Love you."

"Love you too."

I messaged the girls back and told them I could meet around 11. We had coffee and talked about all sorts of things. They were big on the gossip mill. I learned all about Wanda, the bank teller who was cheating on her husband with Will, the bank manager. They shared the deep, dark secrets of the mayor's son's brush with death after a drug deal gone wrong, details that were never publicized, and some juicy details about Janie, the main pediatrician in town's wife who was a flight attendant. Apparently, her primary flights were to exotic places such as tourist traps in Mexico and she was known to thoroughly enjoy her layovers. They knew everybody's business, and I couldn't help but wonder if I was a topic of conversation when I wasn't sitting at the table. We left *The Beanery* and headed to the local sub shop for a bite to eat. I asked them on the walk if they had heard anything more about Shelly. I was hesitant, but I figured if they were comfortable enough to air the rest of the town's dirty laundry then they'd be alright with my inquiry. Marie could hardly wait to speak. She looked at Melinda and rolled her eyes and started right in.

"Well girl, I figured you had heard. She has straight went off the deep end now. The police were called to her apartment to do a welfare check. Apparently, no one had seen her leave her apartment for weeks and so her neighbors contacted the landlord. The landlord went to her apartment and knocked several times with no answer. Finally, he grabbed a master key and opened the door. Once he made it in, he searched through her apartment but did not see her anywhere. He approached the bedroom and found the door closed. He knocked and called out, asking if she was in there and if she was okay. Apparently after a few minutes she quietly responded through the door, "I'm good. Now leave me alone." So, the landlord respected her wishes, locked the apartment back up, and in the vein of extreme caution, called the police. When they arrived, they broke the lock on the bedroom door and found her naked across the top of her bed, incoherent, and pale. They called the squad and had her evaluated. This was about a week ago, and to my understanding, she's being held on the psychiatric floor at *Fary Banks Hospital.*"

"Holy shit! I was just expecting you to say something like she was still pining after Jeff. Does Jeff know?"

Melinda chimed in at this point. "I don't think so. Our men haven't said anything to us. We heard the story from Sophie, the Sheriff's wife."

"I'll tell Jeff. He deserves to know. But Dear Lord. What's next with her?"

Melinda and Marie assured me that Shelly wouldn't cause any problems with the wedding approaching. Marie said she was all bark and no bite. We continued to talk over lunch, and we finished up and said our goodbyes just before two. I took the extra couple of hours before meeting Jeff at home for dinner to taxi out to *Johnson's Farm* to get a little shooting practice in. Jim met me at the gate and smiled big. He'd grown to really like me and seemed to find joy in my visits. He watched as I shot and hit target after target.

"Little lady, you sure are a sharpshooter. I wouldn't have reckoned you'd be this good based on our first meeting, but I sure as Hell wouldn't want to meet up with you in a dark alley." He laughed and smiled at me. I stayed for about an hour and then thanked

227

him and called for a cab back to town. I made it back around 4:30 p.m. and I ordered our Thai food on the way. The taxi dropped me off right in front of the café and I managed to grab the food and make it back to the apartment with about five minutes to spare. I set out some place settings and grabbed two wine glasses and a bottle of red. Jeff walked in about 10 minutes later and I was already sitting on the patio at the table. I decided to surprise him by undressing for dinner. So here I sat, completely naked, glass of wine in hand, Thai food on the table ready to eat, and I could tell with one look that Jeff wasn't hungry for dinner even in the slightest.

"Well, I came home in a bad mood, but I have no idea now what I was even going to start complaining about. We'll eat this later."

He picked me up from the chair and placed me on the lounger. He unzipped his pants, and I leaned up and ripped the belt from his jeans. He was moving slowly, which was totally his style, and usually I appreciated it, but I wanted him now! I felt a little uncomfortable because I knew I should tell him about Shelly, but this just didn't seem like the time. It would kill the mood. I decided to wait until after or maybe even tomorrow morning to spring the news on him. After all, what would one more day hurt? I ripped off his shirt, buttons and all, and he kicked his pants and boxers the rest of the way off as I forcefully pulled him on me. It wasn't a lengthy, intimate encounter, but it was a lustful and erotic sexual experience.

Afterwards we were naked on the patio. The sun was still out. We weren't sure if anyone could see us, and we didn't care. Jeff left for a moment to heat up the Thai food and brought it out to the patio with two new chilled glasses of wine. I sipped as he fed me small tastes of fried rice and beef. Still in this love trance I prayed hard that every day would be like this. I worried that no one deserved to be this happy, but again, I wasn't going to spend useless time questioning it. I gently swallowed each bite that was offered and stared deep into the eyes of what I believed to be my Prince Charming. It was a perfect day for me and an even more perfect evening. I hated to ruin the mood with the sordid information on Shelly, but I honestly felt I didn't have much of a choice. Jeff had different plans though.

Once we were done with the first few bites of food, he scooped me back up and carried me into the shower. He was gentle and it was exhilarating to say the least. He washed every square inch of my body with intricacy. He then grabbed a fresh towel and wrapped me in it. We walked back out to the patio and grabbed our plates of now cold Thai food and one more glass of wine and snuggled up with the rest of our dinner on the lounger where we had just made love an hour earlier. I fed him an eggroll and he gave me bites of the Crab Rangoon. We continued to take turns feeding each other, now sipping wine out of the same glass, and stealing kisses in between bites. The sun started to set, and we fell asleep outside with the warm breeze hitting our face, intertwined in one another.

The next morning came with a sprinkling of rain, and we woke to the droplets hitting our bodies and eye lashes. We laughed and just sat there in the rain; it was as if the new day was cleansing us and inviting us to experience it. It was lovely. When we finally decided to go inside, Jeff went to grab some lattes and pastries from the coffee shop, and I went in to straighten myself up for the day.

Once Jeff returned, we ate our breakfast and afterwards we planned on going out to do some minor tasks for the wedding. I was eager to just go and get things done, but I knew it was time to tell him. "Jeff, I need to tell you something I was told yesterday. I planned on letting you know when you returned home yesterday, but things progressed quickly, if you know what I mean, and it just didn't seem like the time for talking."

"What is it darlin? You seem mighty serious."

"Well, while I was at lunch with Marie and Melinda, they started gossiping about everyone in town. Fortunately, I didn't know most of the people they were spilling tea about, but I inquired about Shelly. I asked straightforwardly if they had heard from her or anything of the sort. I know I should have left her out of the conversation, but you know I have nerves about her and our upcoming nuptials, so I went for it. After asking, they both looked shocked and then turned and started rattling off about her not leaving her apartment and the landlord getting involved and then the police. The talking between the two was chaotic. After a bunch of useless banter, I figured out that, long story short, Shelly had ended up in the hospital and because of the state she was in, they apparently placed her on a psychiatric hold. My understanding is she is still being held and she's been there for over a week. I know you aren't family to her anymore, but should you or we do something?"

Jeff just shook his head and said, "Jessica." He continued to shake his head and say the name, Jessica, under his breath.

Realizing already that Jessica was someone significant in his life before me, I wanted to use caution in my reactions, so I played dumb and pretended that this was the first time I had heard the name.

"Who's Jessica?"

"Jessica was the only other woman I have been serious about besides you and Shelly. Jessica and I got close and then Shelly pulled this bullshit. I fell into the trap and spent weeks going back and forth to the hospital, neglecting Jessica in the process. She was understanding, but eventually grew tired of Shelly's antics; especially after Shelly was released and new bullshit surfaced. Jessica was so in love with me, and I loved her too, but she just couldn't handle it. And she couldn't handle staying here in this little town, still in love with me, but separate from me, and she refused to stay in a relationship that involved another woman constantly interfering. And my work schedule at the lighthouse was on one week and off the next. I was rarely with her because it seemed that Shelly's issues would always arise on the off week. She just couldn't take it, and honestly, I didn't blame her. So, Jessica left town, going on 22 years now. I tried to reach out to her and convince her to stay, but she just couldn't handle it. I understand if you want to go."

"Jeff, I'm not going anywhere. I'm not concerned about her ruining our relationship, but I am worried about the constant stress she's putting on you. What should we do?"

"We should do nothing at all, but I think we will stop by the hospital on our way to do the wedding errands, and we will face this straight off. Tell her that no matter what craziness she pulls, it's NEVER going to work. Now if she's still on the psychiatric floor, it's family only so we will have to wait. If she's been moved, we'll handle this today. And as far as Jessica, we both have loved other people in our past. She sounds like a great person. I'll just leave it at that."

"If you think that's best, sure. We'll go see her. And thanks for not making a big deal over Jessica. She was a great girlfriend and a better woman. It just didn't work out."

We decided to stop by the hospital on the way back in an effort not to taint the wedding plans with a cloud of negativity. We stopped by the flower shop first to check on the order. I had ordered sunflowers, as those were my favorite. Sunflowers are notorious for holding heavy weight while still standing tall and strong and accepting the love of the sun. I resonate with the sunflower, so I found it only proper to have them grace my wedding. My bouquet was made of red roses with one white rose in the center. Red roses symbolize love, but the single white rose is representative of friendship and hence, the central piece to a good relationship and marriage. The sunflowers would line the aisle, which would only have about three rows for the very few friends we were including in our special day. Jeff's boutonniere was being made of one white rose and a sprig of red accent. It was going to be exactly how I wanted it, and I was overjoyed by the florist's attention to my vision. After we completed the flower order and approved the selection, we headed to the bakery. Donna had owned the *Fary Banks Bakery* for over 40 years now and was the go-to woman for all things cake and dessert. I had contacted Donna a month or so ago and shared with her my wishes. She had made a small-scale of the cake I had described, and it was gorgeous. It had two layers of white cake with almond icing. It was lined in strands of pearls and white roses. On top was a sunflower, very elegant, and an anchor inscribed within the flower design. Jeff was my anchor, and I was his. The symbolism was perfect. As far as a reception, we didn't really see the need for one. We decided to have a small gathering on our patio afterwards with wine and fresh Maine lobster, vegetables, whipped potatoes, and of course, our cake. *Annie's Bistro* was going to oversee the dinner. We made a quick stop at *Annie's* to confirm the food order and to settle our bill. We decided to stay for a spell at the Bistro and have a light lunch. Everything was on track and surprisingly, we felt no stress whatsoever. As we were finishing up our lunch, I heard a familiar voice. Every hair stood up on my body and shivers quite literally shot down my spine. It couldn't be. It just couldn't. It was Max.

Chapter 21-Conflict and Resolution

Standing 6 foot 4 and just as handsome as I had remembered him, my ex-husband Max stood there, smiling, right dead center of the bar. I was speechless. Max moved toward me and spoke with that deep voice that could literally melt butter. I cringed. We hadn't even headed off the Shelly situation yet and now this.

"Hey there sweet thing. It's been way too long. You look great. Now don't be rude. Introduce me to your friend."

I started to stutter a bit. "Um, Max. This is my fiancé, Jeff. Jeff, this is um, Max. "

Jeff stood up and stuck his right hand out to shake Max's hand. "Jeff Linford. Great to meet your acquaintance. I've heard a bit about you. So, you're the ex-husband. Great! I'm assuming you're not here to help with the wedding preparations, so what brings you to our little neck of the woods?"

Max snickered. I was still silent. I honestly didn't know what to say. Why in the world would he be here? I hadn't spoken to him in over twenty years. He had zero interest in me or my feelings for the bulk of our marriage. Certainly, he wasn't here because he was interested in me now. And it wouldn't matter if he was. I was in love with Jeff, and I wasn't about to let him ruin things for us. Max looked like he was itching to say something as he moved in even closer to me. He grabbed my hand, pulled me from the bar stool to my feet, and pulled me physically closer to him.

"Alicia, I just wanted to see you. I've been calling, leaving messages, and you never return my calls." He then pulled me to his face, dipped me back, and kissed me. I jerked back immediately. "What in the actual Hell are you doing? Get your hands and your lips off me, Max." He let go and stepped back.

"Awe, come on. It's not like we're strangers."

Jeff cut in at this point. "Max, I have no problem with you being here or even greeting Alicia. I'm confident enough in how I please her to know that you're not competition to me, but if she doesn't want your advances, you best step back and leave her alone."

Max looked less than pleased. "Well, Jeff. It is Jeff, isn't it? Alicia is a big girl. She can speak for herself. And I don't really appreciate having another man tell me what I can or can't do with my wife."

That was it. I was no longer speechless.

"I am not your wife! I was barely your wife when I was married to you. I cannot for the life of me figure out why you would show up after all this time, unless of course you heard I was happy and wanted to try your best to ruin it, but because we do not have any common friends or acquaintances anymore, it seems close to impossible for that to be the case. So, what are you doing here? Speak quickly and then get the Hell out of Fary Banks. We, I mean I, do not want you here! And I never received any phone calls or messages from you. I changed my phone number once I moved away from New Jersey. I wanted to cut ALL ties with my past life, especially you, and until now, I've been quite successful."

"First off, Alicia, I can be wherever I want to be. You don't own the town or this bar. I just wanted to see you. I miss you. I might even still love you."

Jeff moved in. "Okay, that's just about enough..." but before he could finish his statement, Max grabbed ahold of his shoulder and pushed him back. I was having major Deja vu. It wasn't that long ago since

Shelly and I had a similar confrontation, and I wasn't about to have this bullshit repeat itself. I hopped in between them before either of them could get a punch in.

"Stop it! Both of you, just stop it!" Jeff raised his hand up and back. "I'm heading back to the apartment. You two figure out whatever this is that's going on and then Alicia, you can meet me back there once you're finished."

"Jeff, wait. I don't want you to leave." He continued to walk away and out the front door of the bar. Max screamed, "Just let him go. I'm sure he has some important stuff to do back at your apartment." Half laughing, Max shook his head and turned to face me again. I looked at him sternly. "Listen, Max, say what you've come to say and get your ass out of here. I mean it! I'm not putting up with your shit anymore. I'm happy. Jeff makes me happy. You don't. You never did. And you don't want me anyway. You've somehow caught wind of my happiness here, I have no idea how, but I'm sure your primary motivation is to come here and ruin it. So, say it. And move on."

"Alicia, I'm not coming here to stir up any shit. I wanted to see you. I have been calling you. It always went straight to voicemail. It never said it had been disconnected. I had no idea that you had switched phone numbers. I thought you were just ignoring me. I started to worry. I didn't know you were engaged. I didn't know anything about what you were doing here at all. I'm not happy about it, but I didn't know. I just wanted to talk. I know I was wrong. I shouldn't have hurt you the way I did. I shouldn't have been unfaithful. I shouldn't have left you waiting every night, wondering where I was and when I'd return. I can't take it back. I would if I could, but I can't. I just want another chance. You can't be serious about this new guy, Jeff. He's not even your type."

"Max, you don't know my type, obviously. I don't want you here. I loved you for a long time, but eventually I fell out of love. I learned that I deserved better. I decided that being alone was better than feeling alone with you. Jeff is perfect for me. He loves me in a way that I could never have imagined I could be loved. I will NOT allow you to pull into town and ruin things just long enough to draw me back in and then throw me away like yesterday's garbage. I won't even give you the chance. Have a drink, a nice meal, and then get back in whatever brought your sorry ass here and head back to Jersey. That's it! I have nothing else to say to you."

He grabbed at my arm again, trying to pull me closer, but I ripped my body from his reach. I grabbed my purse and ran out of the bar as fast as I possibly could. I ran as best as I could in my sandals and made it back to our apartment in less than five minutes, which was a feat for a ten-minute walk. I busted through the door and didn't even give Jeff a chance to speak. I just ran to him and wrapped my arms around him.

"Please don't be mad, Jeff. I love you. I don't know why he's here, or even how he knew I lived in this town, but I told him to go and hopefully he will."

"I'm not mad at you. I'm not going to lie though, I'm not happy that he's here. We'll figure it out. Between Shelly and Max, I've had enough bullshit for a lifetime, but I love you. I love us. And we'll be fine."

We made it through the evening without hearing from or seeing Max, thankfully. Around 9 p.m. I looked up at Jeff, almost terrified. SHIT! We didn't go see Shelly."

Max leaned up and half grinned at me. "She'll be there tomorrow. We'll go pay her a visit then. Too much excitement for one day already." I nodded agreeingly and placed my head back on his chest. We stayed in and just watched some more black and white movies with wine in our bed. We were notorious for being able to crawl into our happy spaces and block out the world: The patio, the windowsill, the black and white movies, and of course the nook in between his chest and arm were all happy spaces that we both could safely retreat to escape the outside world. We fell asleep early, in each other's arms.

The next morning, we showered and drank our coffee as usual. I had another shooting lesson, and I was concerned that I wasn't going to be able to escape for four hours without Jeff being suspicious.

So, I decided to fess up. He deserved to know anyway.

"Jeff, I have plans today. I know we need to stop by the hospital to deal with Shelly, but I've been doing something sort of secretive the past few months. It's not bad, and as much I as hate omissions, it was more of an omission than a lie."

Jeff looked frighteningly concerned. "What is it?"

"Well, I've been taking shooting lessons. Target practice. I've owned a gun for years. Daddy gave it to me when I was younger. I started to feel unsafe when Shelly kept making her threats and then it occurred to me that I've been living here all this time with no real way to protect myself. You moved in and obviously I felt safer, but I thought, what could it hurt? You like shooting and so I figured eventually it would be something we could have in common and do together. So, I have a lesson this afternoon and I didn't want to have any more secrets between us, especially after Max showing up yesterday. I didn't want to disappear for several hours and have you wondering if I was with him."

"Darlin, it's not a big deal. I wish you had told me sooner, but this omission seems harmless, unless of course you're plotting to shoot me," he snickered.

"No sir. Just wanted to feel more confident. So, do you want to go with me today? Maybe stop by the hospital and then head out to *Johnson's Farm?*"

"Sounds like a plan to me. Let's get dressed and head out."

We got ourselves together and took a cab to the hospital. As we approached the front desk, I noticed a tall, dark-haired man in a suit leaning over the counter at the nurse's station. I was confident I had seen that ass before. I walked closer and leaned around the front of the station and there he was again. It was Max.

"Max, what in the Hell are you doing here?"

"Hi ya Alicia. Odd seeing you here. I'm just here to visit a friend."

Before I could say anything else to him, the cute little blonde nurse said follow me, and escorted him towards a patient room. I followed slowly behind to see that he entered room 136.

I hustled back to Jeff's side and looked at him, awe-struck. "What in the actual Hell is going on here?" Jeff just shrugged and asked the front desk for Shelly Linford's room. The lady behind the desk looked up and said, "Certainly. She's been a busy bee this morning. Room 136." "Jeff, that's the room Max just entered. There's NO WAY that they know each other." Jeff's face grew red and angered. "Come with me. We're about to find out."

I felt like I was walking the plank as I headed down the narrow hallway of patient rooms. Nurses were laughing and talking. Doctors were reiterating patient notes to other nurses. The fluorescent lights were flickering, and I could hear them slowly buzzing. Random hospital machines were beeping. My ADHD was overloaded. I felt as if I was going to pass out. My hand grew limp as we approached room 136. It was sweaty and I lost Jeff's grip and slowly dropped to the floor in the doorway.

"Nurse, somebody come and help me, please. I think my fiancé just fainted."

I could hear Jeff calling for help. I could still hear the beeping and buzzing and talking, but I couldn't open my eyes and I couldn't say a word. I heard a nurse say to grab an IV bag and another ask for help lifting me to a bed. I felt the prick of the needle in my arm, and I could feel the cool liquid slowly move through my veins. It seemed like hours, but probably just moments later, I opened my eyes and saw Jeff standing above me.

"Welcome back my love. I guess all of this was too much for you, because you just dropped like a fly right in the entryway of the room."

I looked to my left and there she was, Shelly lying in the hospital bed next to me. Max was sitting in the chair to the left of her bed. I thought to myself, this is exactly what Hell must feel like. I was overwhelmed. I closed my eyes and dozed back off. They must have given me something to calm me in the IV because when I woke again, an entire day had passed.

I looked up again to see Jeff sitting next to my bed. He was wearing the same clothing, so I assumed he hadn't left my side. That made me a bit uncomfortable because I feared what might have been said between him and Shelly while I was out. I did notice that Max was no longer in the room.

"Hey Darlin. How are you feeling?"

"I'm okay, I think. I have a bit of a headache, but I'm guessing that's to be expected. We missed our appointment yesterday. Did you call Mr. Johnson?"

"Yes ma'am. Don't worry about anything. I've got everything covered. And Shelly and I had a long conversation. She delved into your history online and found out about Max. She reached out to him. It's been a setup to split us up from the start. He's still in town, but he admitted to the entire thing. I think he plans on leaving soon. He's staying at *Cindy's Bed & Breakfast*. We can pay him a visit once they release you."

"So, what did they say was wrong with me?"

"They assume it was the combination of stress, not eating enough, and the red wine the night before. The combination caused your blood pressure to be offset. Nothing serious. You just need to make sure you're eating enough."

"Okay. Good. And I see she's resting peacefully. What did she agree to exactly?"

"Well, I basically told her that she would stop the shit, or I'd hire a lawyer and file a restraining order. She wants to be able to be in our lives on some level and a restraining order would make that incredibly difficult. I think she'll back off and calm down now. At least I hope she will. Let me go get the nurse, have them get you a bite to eat, and see if we can get you discharged and out of this room with her."

Jeff left the room briefly and I could see that Shelly was tossing around in the bed next to me. I believed she hadn't been asleep, but rather listening in on our conversation. She rolled over and said "Hey."

"Hey." That's honestly all I could mutter back to her.

"Alicia, I'm sorry. I get crazy when it comes to Jeff. I never fully got over him. I drank too much and took a few sleeping pills and sadly didn't wake up for days. When they brought me to the hospital, they didn't have to pump my stomach or anything like that. Enough time had passed, and I was still stable, but I admitted to what I had done and that I had done it before. After the mandatory three-day hold, I asked to stay to attend some counseling and therapy sessions. They just brought me to a regular room yesterday morning, just a few hours before you and Jeff arrived. I reached out to your ex in a last-ditch attempt to break you two up. I made contact a few days before I overdosed. When he didn't respond, I began to feel like the walls were closing in. Apparently, he did respond, but the email went to spam. We didn't even have a formal plan. I think he just came because he hadn't been able to reach you and he was curious. I doubt he'll cause any real problems. It's my fault. All of it. And I promise I'll butt out of your relationships. I would like to eventually be friends."

"Okay. Okay. Shelly this is way too much way too quickly. I think..." Jeff came back in with the head nurse.

"Hello, Alicia. I'm going to take some vitals quickly and then send you home with an anxiety prescription and get you out of here. Sound good?"

"Yes, ma'am. Thank you."

She took the vitals, and everything seemed to be normal; I mean the vitals were normal, but clearly not my life. Jeff sat me up and helped me get my clothing back on. The nurse brought in a wheelchair, per hospital requirements, and she wheeled me out of room 136, hopefully forever. Once we were home, I felt awkward and uncomfortable in my own apartment. For some reason, I did not feel that strong, loving pull towards Jeff. I was certain it was just the stress of the entire situation, but I felt nothing, just numb. He reached for my hand, and I pulled away without even thinking about the reaction.

"What is it, Darlin? What's wrong?"

"Nothing, Jeff. I just need a little space. It's been a strange and stressful couple of days, wouldn't you agree?"

"Yes, for us both. And I thought maybe being closer to each other would help us get through the emotions and confusion, but if you need space, take it."

"I'm sorry. Just for a little bit, if that's okay. I'll just go and sit in the window in the room. Maybe make me a cup of coffee?"

"Sure, Darlin. Whatever you need."

Chapter 22-Changing Lanes

Several days passed and Jeff and I had barely spoke, much less touched each other. He smiled and brushed my shoulder when he walked by, but I had asked for space, and he apparently was giving it to me. I wasn't upset with him. I was just upset. I didn't feel safe in my own home, and that was a feeling I couldn't get used to. I hopped in the shower because honestly, I couldn't remember my last one. I'm guessing it was the morning of the hospital fiasco, so I was on like day four of a messy bun. I washed my hair and shaved everything. I then turned my back towards the hot water spraying down over my head and back and just stood there. It felt good and I needed to just let everything go. I began to cry. Sob. I screamed a little and collected myself so that Jeff wouldn't come in and interrupt the emotional breakdown that I clearly deserved. I got it all out. All of it. And then I turned off the shower, draped a towel around my hips, and moved towards the bedroom to make love to my fiancé, because it was time.

Jeff looked shocked as I walked across the bedroom floor, seductive and apparently ready to minimize the space between us. He had already showered and was sitting on the bed in his boxer shorts. I crawled from the end of the bed up to the top where he was. I slid up on top of him and took note of the scar on his chest again; a scar we had never discussed. I had seen him naked more times than I could count, and it never came up? So, I paused in my seductive pursuit and asked him.

"Jeff, what is this scar from?"

"I wondered when you were going to ask. You've traced it with your finger a dozen times. You've always seemed intrigued by it. But you've never asked, so I just never said anything. It's from Desert Storm. I served from 1988 to 1996. Then when the towers fell, I volunteered to go back. It was brutal. My third tour just about did me in. My age was the biggest factor; I wasn't in the best shape to be shipping out, but I was so angered by it all, I just had to do something. So, I did, and while I was there, my unit was struck by a roadside bomb. Luckily, none of us were killed, but two of the men lost an arm and one had to have a foot amputated. I was lucky. I just took shrapnel to the chest. The three severely injured were sent home. The rest of us stayed until our tour was complete. Once a Marine, always a Marine, but I don't talk about my third tour there. Most of that shit just can't be unseen. I don't have what I'd call PTSD, but I still have nightmares occasionally."

It was odd to me that we hadn't even discussed his service or being a Marine before now. That's something most Marines are so proud of that it essentially becomes a lifestyle. Jeff wasn't like other men though. He wasn't prideful or arrogant. I do remember a young gentleman walking up to us in the hardware store and saying, "Semper Fi" to Jeff. Apparently he was aware of his service. Then we became distracted by someone else, and the conversation never came up. I felt guilty that I hadn't shown interest; not even enough to ask him to elaborate after that interaction. I felt a sense of guilt, but also of pride. As if he wasn't hot enough. Now a war hero too. I'm not sure what I did to deserve this man, but I intended to let him know how much I loved and appreciated him. I turned my focus back to Jeff.

"I'm sorry I never asked before. I should have known, I guess."

"Darlin, it was a long time ago. I should have shared some of my past with you. It's just that so much of my past has already caused you pain; I thought maybe you'd heard enough for now. Anyway, now that you know, can we get back to you loving on me?" He giggled a little and seemed unbothered by the brief discussion of his service. I smiled and continued halfway up the length of his body.

"Sure." But I was distracted. This man had been through more than I could even imagine. Just horrific things between his military service, and Shelly, and Jessica, and God knows what else he has yet to tell me. I shook it off. We needed each other. And so, I crawled the rest of the way up, traced the scar tenderly on his chest, and we made love. Afterwards, we laid there for a while, just staring at the ceiling. I think we both just had to take everything in and find a way to let it all go. After about an hour, I decided it was time to rejoin the world. "Let's go get something for lunch, stop by and make sure Max has left, and maybe go on out to the farm and see if he can squeeze us in for some practice. Then maybe tonight, we could go see a movie and take a walk on the beach...get back to feeling normal?"

"Sounds good to me. Let me throw on some clothes and we'll head out."

The Bed & Breakfast that Max was staying at had a quaint little restaurant inside, so we decided to kill two birds with one stone and grab a bite there. They had delicious croissants with fresh tuna or chicken salad and fresh cut fruit. Their chips were house made, crispy and delicious. We had a wonderful, quiet lunch on the terrace and then asked the lady at the front desk if Max was still staying with them. Normally this information would be taboo to give out to the public, but Jeff knew everybody in town, and she seemed at ease sharing details with him. After reviewing her computer, she found that he was in fact still here and she asked us to take a seat while she called him down. We waited for about 20 minutes before Max surfaced. He walked down the curved stairs looking sexy as hell per usual. It made me sick to my stomach to see him, but his attractiveness could not be denied or unfortunately, ignored.

"Well, if it isn't the Mr. and almost Mrs. here to visit me. What do I owe this honor? I'm certain I was told to stay away from Alicia, so why did you bring her here to see me, Jeff?"

"We just wanted to make sure you were on your way out soon."

"Well, it's really none of your business, now, is it? It's perfectly legal for me to travel. To visit Fary Banks. To stay at a Bed & Breakfast. I'm certain I do not need either of your permission to do any of these things. And after visiting, I've got to say, I'm impressed with this little town. Maybe enough to stay. I've been wanting to leave the corporate life and big city living behind me for quite some time. Maybe Fary Banks is the puzzle piece I've been searching for."

I legitimately thought I was going to vomit. "Max. You can't do this to me! It's not fair! You hurt me so many times and I have asked nothing of you. Can't you respect me enough to let me be? I'll never be at peace if you're here."

"Your peace comes from within you. It has nothing to do with me."

My eyes almost rolling out of my head, "Boy, Max, that's quite philosophical. Have you been watching the daytime talk shows again on DVR while you lie lonely in your bed thinking about the life you threw away?"

Wow, I thought to myself. That's the first time I had ever stood up to him. Not sure where it came from, but I was impressed with myself, if even for a minute. I became increasingly worried though that Jeff might think I was regretting the life I tossed to the side so many years ago, even if warranted. So, I stepped back and shut up.

Max almost snickering again with that obnoxiously handsome coy smile rebutted, "I'm not saying I'm moving here. I'm just saying I might, and I can if I want to. Maybe I'll hook up with that sweet little thing you threw to the wayside, Shelly."

I seriously thought Jeff was going to explode. The shade of red his face turned was like nothing I had ever seen before. The look in his eyes was unrecognizable. I was starting to wonder about the rage that grew inside him. Maybe this military thing was something we needed to discuss a little further. Whatever it was, his reaction was not normal. He charged at Max, and I did my best to jump in between them, but as I did, Jeff raised his left arm and shoulder and accidentally clipped me in the face knocking me to the ground. I was stunned more than hurt, but I stayed down. Me falling and getting hurt didn't stop him. He punched Max with his other fist and then continued barreling towards him in a fury until Max's suit was covered in blood and his nose clearly broken. At that point Jeff snapped back. The hate left his eyes and expression. He looked sad. Broken-hearted. He dropped to his knees and scooped me up into his arms, cradling me like a baby.

"Alicia, I am so sorry. I don't know what came over me. I mean, I do, but I didn't intend to hurt you. I didn't intend to hurt Max. I don't give a shit if he's here or if he screws around with Shelly. I do care that his presence hurts you. Let me look at your cheek." He then looked over to the front desk and asked the lady to call 911 to get Max an ambulance or at least some medical care. The lady did as she was told, probably because she was afraid of Jeff, and then knelt with some towels to put pressure on Max's nose and to absorb some of the blood. Max said nothing. He just stayed on the ground holding his nose. I guess he was done with arrogance and confrontation for the day. And though it hurt me to see Max injured, it hurt me more to know that my future husband was capable of snapping like that and then acting as if he had no real recollection of what had just come over him. It had to be related to his service. It just had to be. Out of fear and concern, I decided to tread lightly and say nothing at all.

Jeff asked for a bag of ice and then placed it on my cheek. He caressed my face and brushed the loose strands of hair out of the way. Strangely, this was the first time I had felt safe in over a week and that was odd with what I just saw. He said very little. Just held me and continued to caress my face. When the ambulance and police arrived, the police took a statement from each of us and then told us that they'd be in touch. Apparently, Max had decided not to press charges. I didn't tell the police how I hurt my face because I didn't want to chance Jeff getting in any trouble. And for the second time this week, our plans for the day had been screwed up by the notorious exes. Obviously, I didn't feel like shooting with G.I. Joe, so I asked if we could just go home, but the sadness in Jeff's eyes overcame me. Somehow, even though all of this was his fault, I still felt sorry for him. I mean, yes, Max played a huge role, but Jeff must be held accountable for his own actions. And I didn't want to mother him. And of course, I felt some guilt over my reaction to Shelly. I mean I didn't have any affiliation with the military, and I still threw hands at her. I'm no different. I shouldn't be judging Jeff or his reaction to Max at all, but the reality of the situation was that I was incapable of hurting Jeff, but he was fully capable of hurting me and quite possibly wouldn't have any recollection of it. I decided still to remain calm and act unbothered as to avoid upsetting him any further.

"What do you want to do, Jeff? If you don't want to go home, I'll go in the restroom here and freshen up."

"I think we need some time away. How about I book something on the Cape, and we can spend the next few days there just relaxing and escape the bullshit that seems to be chasing us around Fary Banks. I'll book us a suite facing the ocean and we'll schedule a couple's massage. You can have some pampering done and we'll eat dinner on the beach. Just us. No distractions."

I looked up at him and smiled. The smile was a little forced, but it was a smile, nonetheless.

"Honestly, that sounds good. I could use a few days away from everything. Let's do it."

Jeff grabbed his cell phone and made a few calls and then looked at me lovingly.

"No need to pack anything. We'll pick up whatever we need there. Clothes, toiletries, whatever. I'll take care of it. I rented us a car and they're dropping it off here. I'll go order a few cappuccinos and we can go outside and wait for them to get here."

"Okay. I'll be outside on the bench."

About the time I made it to the bench, they were rolling Max outside to take him to the hospital to get an x ray and some pain medication, I assume. He looked over at me and stared with the most frightening glare. I simply nodded and then looked away. He has no right to be upset with me. I was trying to finally live my best life here with Jeff and then he decided to come and stir shit up. That's on him. I've had enough, and honestly, I was eager to get the hell out of Fary Banks.

Chapter 23-The Cape

A newer model convertible pulled up to the B & B and a rental truck followed behind it. A nice gentleman stepped out of the convertible, handed a document to sign and the keys to Jeff, and then he returned to the rental truck and rode off. Jeff opened the door for me, and I settled into the front seat. Jeff got in on the driver's side and said, "Buckle up baby. We're off to the Cape. Nothing to even think about for at least four days. But do keep the ice pack on your cheek for a little longer. Don't want it to swell or bruise if we can avoid it."

It was about a four-hour drive to the resort where Jeff booked our stay. I had never just picked up and left before, other than when I made the move to get away from Max, so I was feeling a little bit anxious. My mind was secretly racing, and I felt an overwhelming sense of guilt over the Max drama, especially since I chose not to share how serious the issues were in our marriage with Jeff prior to his surprise visit.

After about thirty minutes of silence, Jeff looked over at me and I decided to bring up the elephant in the car.

"Jeff, do you think that maybe we should procrastinate the wedding until late Spring? It would be plenty warm on the water in mid-May, and it would give us time to ward off all the negativity. It's our schedule, not everyone else's. Most people do not even know that we're getting married, so no one will think anything of us postponing."

"What about the food and flowers and the cake? We've already arranged and paid for all of this."

"I'll call them, give them the new dates, and I'm sure they will all be fine with it. I just want the dust to settle a little with Shelly and Max. I want our special day to be perfect. What do you think?"

"I think that I just want you to be happy and if that will make you happy, then I say let's do it. I don't care when I marry you, or where I marry you, just so you become my wife. We could hop a plane to Vegas, and I'd be happy, but I think as much sadness as we've experienced in our past relationships, that a perfect day for us both is in order, and so let's just move the date. Make the calls if you feel like it. We've got a way to go before we get to the resort anyway."

I smiled and did my usual consenting nod, and then started searching up the numbers on my phone to make the necessary adjustments to our wedding plans. I texted Marie and Melinda too, so they'd know. I really didn't have anyone else I needed to inform. Once the plans were settled, I nuzzled back into my seat. The top was down, and as the salty wind blew through my hair I began to relax and took a nap. I needed the rest after everything, and the sun beating down combined with the light breeze made the conditions perfect. Jeff had slow jazz lightly playing on the radio and for just a few moments, I felt complete peace within.

I woke from my nap to a loud thump. Must have been a pothole, but it roused me. "Everything okay?"

"Yep, just a rough patch in the road. How was your nap? We're almost there; probably another 30 minutes or so. Are you hungry or would you like to wait until we arrive? I was going to stop about an hour back, but you were resting so peacefully, I hated to wake you."

"I slept fine. No, I'm good. We can grab a bite at the resort."

The scenery was just beautiful. I could see the ocean, waves crashing up on the beach, and little kids tossing beach balls. Their parents were scattered across the sand, lying on the beach in sun chairs with umbrellas peppering the land. It seemed a teensy bit warmer here than at home. I loved the sun beating down on my skin; though I did have a moment of concern because we had been driving for almost four hours with the top down and I didn't have a lick of sunscreen on, nor did I have any with me. I was prone to skin cancer, and I had never mentioned this to Jeff, so I found it to probably be an inopportune time to bring it up considering all the recent details I had shielded him from. No need to create another thing for him to worry about right now. I guess it is what it is.

Moments later, we pulled up to a long driveway that directed us up the hillside, lined in wildflowers and beautiful foliage. I could see the top of the resort on the hillside; white pillars and soft pastels accenting the windows. The site alone was enough to take my breath away.

"It's just lovely here, Jeff."

"I thought you would like it. I saw an advertisement for this place several months back. I initially thought it would be a nice interlude to a larger honeymoon, but I think maybe we need it more now than later."

"I couldn't agree more."

Once we arrived, we parked the car and walked through the large entryway, also lined with delicate flowers and flowering shrubs. I could smell lavender, and the fragrance overwhelmed my senses, bringing a serenity that was necessary after the last few weeks.

Jeff grabbed my hand and guided me through the entrance as we approached the concierge. "Good afternoon. We have a suite reserved for Linford."

"Perfect," the young lady said. "Your room is room 136, beachfront."

We both looked at each other in dismay. "Room 136?" I spoke up.

"Ma'am, do you buy chance have another beachfront suite with a different room number? I'd rather not explain, but I really would like to avoid staying in room 136."

"Let me check." She punched in several things in her computer and looked up with a smile. Certainly. Here are your keys, Mr. and Mrs. Linford. Room 148, oceanfront.

I thanked her and didn't bother correcting her assumption that we were married. We both liked the sound of it anyway. We continued up to our room, ordered room service with champagne and a light lunch, and then hopped in the shower to wash the day off us. Once we finished showering, Jeff brought me in a linen robe that the hotel had provided for us. We put the robes on and went out onto the terrace, facing the beach until the food arrived. Several moments later we heard a knock on the door. "Room service." Jeff went to the door, thanked and tipped the gentleman, and rolled the cart of goodies out onto the terrace. It was late afternoon, and the sun was burning hot. A ceiling fan with leaf shaped blades spun above our head and it provided just enough breeze to keep the sun from frying us. Jeff popped the champagne and poured us both a glass.

He toasted us, "The wait isn't punishment. It's preparation for the love we deserve. Our love is all that matters, and we will make it work, no matter the intrusions, regardless of the cost. You are the light of my life. Everything will work out as it should. I love you, Alicia."

The toast brought me to tears. I couldn't even respond at first. I just leaned in and kissed him softly, then took a sip of my champagne and began nibbling on the spread of food in front of me. Regardless of the disturbing way this week had gone, this moment was perfect, and I fully intended to drink it in.

I winked at him flirtatiously and said, "I guess there's no need to write your vows."

He smiled back and nodded. "I speak the truth, and I fully intend to make you certain of my feelings to the extent that vows won't be necessary. You'll already know."

As the sun began to set, Jeff and I realized we didn't have anything fresh to wear. He threw his jeans and t shirt on and ran down to the resort gift shop where he grabbed a few sundresses for me and a couple of pairs of shorts and t shirts for himself. Luckily, they had flip flops as well for both of us; otherwise, I'd be wearing these clunky tennis shoes for the entire trip. I texted Jeff and asked him to grab some sunscreen and some aloe for the red glow that already embellished my freckled skin from the car ride in. I also reminded him to stop at the front desk for some complimentary toiletries, deodorant, toothpaste, a couple of toothbrushes, and a razor. Luckily, I had a brush, a couple of hair clips, and a travel size perfume already in my purse. I also had my travel makeup bag as I never went anywhere without it. We didn't, however, have phone chargers with us and we weren't expecting the resort to have any, so we accepted that no one would be able to reach us. And this is exactly what we both needed. Complete solitude.

Though the thought messed with my anxiety level a little, I realized that Jeff was the only one I cared about talking to or knowing my whereabouts anyway, so I would be fine. When Jeff made it back to the room, I tossed on the flip flops and sundress and waited for him to change. Then we walked out to the beachfront to take a seat and watch the sunset as the waves crashed in. Jeff had grabbed two glasses and a bottle of red while shopping for incidentals, so he poured us a glass, and we just sat in awe of the view and the time together.

We were fortunate enough to find a couple of bathing suits that fit at the resort shop; though I wasn't even sure if suits were required. I saw many couples scantily dressed; several women who weren't even wearing tops. I guess for the money, the resort just turned a blind eye. We didn't plan anything during this stay. We slept when we wanted and ate when we were hungry. We explored the beauty of the resort, hiking and flouncing in the water. On the 2nd day, Jeff told me to put on my suit and to meet him in the lobby. When I arrived, he had a basket in one hand and a blanket in the other. I didn't even ask what his plans were, I just followed him. I couldn't imagine just blindly following anyone else in my life, but the hold this man had on me was like no other. He was exquisite in any form of the word. I couldn't even spend time worrying about his mild violent streak because I knew it was in protection of me. Or at least that was my hope.

We headed out the main door and down the hill just a bit. Then he pulled me to the right down a cobblestone path that wasn't visible from the main driveway. We walked for about 30 minutes downhill and then made a swift left and then another right uphill for a bit. I was surely regretting the flip flops at this point and then I saw it.

I said nothing. We turned again and descended the hill to the water. An inlet of some sort. And there we were. Standing at the foot of the most beautiful waterfall I had ever seen. Jeff let go of my hand momentarily and spread out the blanket on a small patch of grass close to the sand. He sat down the basket and then said, "Sit."

I complied, obviously. I was once again speechless. Jeff then spread-out napkins and a small plate with fresh fruit, cheese, crackers, and of course, the bottle of red. He had also brought a slice of key lime pie; I assume to share.

We ate our picnic while watching the beautiful waterfall, and I couldn't help but think that things would never get any better than this very moment. I did my best to take it all in. I wanted to have this moment forever etched in my memory so that when and if things were rough between us or even in life in general, I could return to this moment for a sense of peace and happiness.

Once we were finished with our lunch, he grabbed my hand and pulled me to my feet. I think the most erotic part of this experience so far was that he didn't say a word past, "sit." His eyes seduced me. His mouth seduced me. The picnic and the scenery and the planning that it took to arrange this romantic retreat seduced me. And in such a short time frame he managed to pull all of this off. I was a goner, and in the best possible way. I knew I would never feel complete or fulfilled without this man in my life, and that scared me.

Once I was standing, he untied the back of my bikini top and then slid my bottoms off. I stood there motionless; he was in control and clearly wanted to be, so I obeyed.

Slowly he slipped his own trunks off and there we were, standing near a magical waterfall, all alone, exposed but exhilarated. He grabbed my hand and led me towards the waterfall, through the shallow water.

We walked through the sandy, pebbled water to the fall itself. It grew a little deeper at the waterfall, about waist high. And there, under the waterfall, I experienced the most erotic and seductive sexual experience of my life. No concern whatsoever for anyone or anything else. No care that someone from a distance might catch a peek at our lovemaking. As far as we were concerned, it was just us and nature. As God intended.

He went slow, paying attention to all the parts of me that needed it. The water temperature was warm and refreshing at the same time. The waterfall dropped water just behind our bodies as we blended into one person.

I took a moment afterwards, as he was holding me in the water to really appreciate the moment. I did this with every life changing event. I wanted to make a memory. A photograph in my head, just for me. I knew I would never forget how I felt or how he felt inside me. It was stimulating beyond words; every part of me was tingling. And somehow I still yearned for more. We melted into the water and into each other. This was the moment I had been waiting for my entire life, and I couldn't help but think that no one, especially me, was deserving of this level of content and happiness.

Our final evening involved a candlelight dinner on the beach. Jeff had scheduled a spa day for me, and I felt beautiful. I had found a dress in the resort shop that draped all my curves just right. This was so important to me. I always wanted to feel comfortable in my own skin. I wasn't a large woman, but at 5 foot 9 and hips that were a little broader than I had hoped for, I always needed to find just the right dress or pair of jeans that accented the frame God gave me. My chest wasn't large or small, just there, and so I usually tried to accent it with something that lifted my meagre cleavage. This dress did all those things, and what luck, considering my shopping options included just one small gift shop at a secluded resort.

I was excited for him to see me. I quite literally felt like I was floating through the hallway towards the elevator to meet him. I secretly wished we could just stay here forever, but one last evening would have to do.

The dinner was elegant and included fresh seafood, local delicacies, and tantalizing desserts. We had an after-dinner coffee and watched as the sun began to set. Jeff arranged for music to play, and we danced, alone, at the beachfront. We fell asleep for a bit on the beach and awoke to waves crashing and just so gently sprinkling salty water on us. We grabbed our things and headed back to our room, an actual oasis, for one last night of love making without the distraction of anyone or anything else. We woke to the sunrise shining ever so brightly through the window. We went to a couple's massage and one more latte on the veranda and then left the resort at noon, satisfied and exhilarated. This trip could not have been better. It was exactly what we needed, and it reassured me, more now than ever, that Jeff was the one. The only one.

I knew we would have obstacles to overcome and that we still had a lot to learn about each other, but I was positive that no one else would ever bring me the joy and peace that he did. And that was enough for me.

Chapter 24-Back to Reality

It was a Tuesday in early September, and we were both fortunate to have avoided both Shelly and Max for the past few weeks. We heard rumors that Max had put a deposit down on a condo on the East side of town, but we didn't waste any time verifying it. We just didn't care anymore. We were going to live our lives, and everyone else could live theirs. All our wedding coordinators had returned calls and verified the new date, now May 28th, so that was one thing we could scratch off our immediate list of things to worry about. Basically, everything was back to being relatively carefree, and we were good with that. Jeff had to head to the bank to make a deal on another repo project, and I made plans with Marie to have lunch. I was thinking of asking her to go shooting with me this afternoon. I liked her better than Melinda; I felt like we could be good friends without the trio. Jeff was excited for me to venture out a little more and though I think he was a little sad that we hadn't made the time to go shooting together, but I was pleased because I wanted to be prepared to really impress him when we went. I'm certain as prissy as I am, he wasn't expecting too much out of me. The thought made me giggle and blush a little.

I'd been working out regularly too. Obviously, I needed to stay in shape for the wedding in the Spring, and every woman knows that the holidays tend to result in packing on a few pounds just by default, so I wanted to be prepared and a little cautious. It wasn't a revenge body by any means, but I was quite certain I could kick someone's ass if need be. I mentioned asking Marie to go to target practice with me and he explained that from what he understood, Marie was a regular visitor at *Johnson's*

Farm and that she'd probably be thrilled that I wanted her to go with me. Apparently, Melinda is a big gun control fanatic and doesn't think that it's necessary to go and shoot guns, much less own one. I was pleased to hear this tidbit of information in advance. It might have stirred up some real shit if I'd invited her along one day, and that's the last thing I needed...more shit. I grabbed my gun purse, gave Jeff a smooch, and headed out to meet Marie at the bistro for lunch. I noticed Jeff peaking at the bedazzled gun purse as I was leaving. I'm sure he was thinking back to the numerous times I snuck by him and tucked it in my sweater drawer. Never once did he ask why I didn't carry the "supposed" purse to dinner or shopping.

Trust, I thought to myself. He trusts me and doesn't feel the need to ask a bunch of clarifying questions. I guess I was still just trying to get used to that.

When I arrived at the bistro, Marie was already sitting at a bar table having a drink. I walked up and took the empty seat. "Hey girl, what's up?"

Marie smiled. "Hey Alicia. Glad you could make it. I've got a bunch of tea to spill."

Marie was notorious for knowing all the good gossip. I grinned and said, "Spill it."

Marie dove in.

"So, I was at *The Beanery* Saturday, and I was sitting at the front corner table, waiting on Melinda of course, and I overheard Sophie, you know, the Sheriff's wife, carrying on about some big fiasco at the Bed and Breakfast in midtown. Apparently, some "come here" was stirring up shit with a local guy, and his girlfriend got in the middle of the brawl and ended up getting punched in the face."

I could feel my face getting red and flushed. This was the fight that took place weeks ago between Jeff and Max, and apparently no one knew who was involved, just that it happened. So, I decided to play dumb until I could get all the details. Playing along I said, "Continue."

"So, anyway, the lady at the front desk apparently gave a statement to the police and the out of towner requested that no charges be filed, but I guess it was a huge ordeal. Everyone's been talking about it since Sophie spilled the beans."

My mind was racing. Do I tell her? I mean, she is a good friend, I guess, and I don't want her to find out later and think that I lied to her. That damn omission clause gets me every time.

"Well, Marie, I've got to tell you something. I knew about the fiasco because I was the woman that received the punch."

Marie's jaw dropped. She was speechless and I couldn't tell if she was just shocked or irritated because I let her carry on about the whole scene.

"Let me explain better. My ex-husband showed up a few days prior to the incident and stirred up a bunch of shit. Come to find out, he was in cahoots with Shelly." I could tell by Marie's expression she was beyond confused. "I know. I know. How did Shelly end up with my ex? Well, oddly enough, she did some online research and found out about him and his whereabouts. Then she reached out and asked him to come here to interfere with me and Jeff. Their email communications went to her spam folder, so she thought he was ignoring her. She then got desperate and pulled the overdose scheme that apparently she's famous for when things don't go her way. Anyway, he had emailed back, and when Jeff and I went to confront Shelly at the hospital, low and behold, Max was there in her patient room. She looked as shocked as I did. Some words were exchanged, and I became unusually dizzy, a spell of vertigo, and down I went. I was in the hospital for a couple of days and get this...in the same room with Shelly! It was a real cluster of bullshit. After I was sent home, we waited a few days and then went to confront Max at the bed and breakfast. We basically just wanted him to leave us alone and to make sure he didn't intend on staying for any length of time. Max acted as Max always does, cocky and conceited, and then fists started to fly. I was caught in the crossfire. Jeff broke Max's nose and the EMT and police were called. Max decided to cool down and keep his mouth shut, but the lady at the front desk saw everything. I figured it would get out eventually. I'm shocked our names weren't smeared all over town! I didn't tell you because immediately after, Jeff took me away to the Cape for a long weekend. We needed to escape. On the drive there, we decided to postpone the wedding until Spring so we could deal with any Shelly and Max related drama first. Since we've been back, I really haven't spoken to anyone until today. I haven't even had the chance to talk to you about postponing the wedding. I'm sorry. I did send you a text, but I'm sure my service was spotty at the beach."

"Well, that was a plethora of information. Waitress, I think we're going to need the entire bottle." I giggled and she laughed. We were really hitting it off as a duo. I could tell our friendship was going to flourish. I secretly was hoping that she'd prefer me over Melinda but grown women don't often profess things like that. So, I continued to just be me and pray it was enough to keep this new friendship afloat.

I continued the conversation to avoid any awkwardness as we both sat there smiling at each other like fools over the idea of an entire bottle of wine at lunch, which might prove to be a dangerous combination with my afternoon target practice plans, which I had yet to mention to her.

"Anyway, I'm fine. Jeff's fine. Everything is fine. I heard a rumor that Max was buying a condo here, which is inopportune, but it is what it is."

"Okay, girl. That's way too much bullshit for a Tuesday. Just kidding. I'm glad you're okay. Hopefully, this Max person goes back where he came from."

"Yes. Hopefully. Anyway, after lunch I am heading to *Johnson's Farm* for target practice. Jeff said you like to shoot too. Want to go with me?"

"Sure. That sounds like fun. We'd have to swing by my apartment to get my gun."

"Yay. I'll get the check."

"Slow down sis. We've got a half a bottle of red to finish."

So, we drank another glass of wine a piece and finished up our light lunch and headed out the door. I was a little excited to stop at Marie's apartment too. You can tell a lot about a woman by where and how she lives. I was confident she was eloquent in her decorating decisions. Her clothing was always top notch as was her hair and makeup, and her accessories weren't cheap or costume. She exuded confidence and class. I was hopeful that she felt the same about me, though I'm sure she had noticed that many of my accessories were old and cheap looking. I just couldn't part with them. They provided me comfort. They were familiar.

The old, faithful strappy sandals and dad's necklace were staples in my wardrobe. So, I guess our presentation doesn't always tell the whole story.

We took a taxi to Marie's apartment so she could run in quick and grab her gun purse, and I tagged along to do a tad of snooping. We asked the cabby to hang out for a few minutes so we wouldn't have to struggle to find another. Her apartment, as expected, was exquisite. The living room surprisingly had a cathedral style ceiling which is uncommon in apartments in the community we live in, so the rent must be atrocious, and she had the most beautiful fireplace I had ever seen. I didn't get to venture much past the living room and kitchen, but she had pieces displayed that cost much more than my monthly rent, I was sure of it. She had to come from money. Still, I was taken by her. Not jealous, not even envious, but mesmerized by her beauty and clear confidence. Without truly knowing that much about her, she was the epitome of success in my mind, and I yearned to be more like her. To have her certainty and poise.

After she grabbed her gun purse, we hopped back in the cab and headed towards the farm. It took about 35 minutes to get there from Marie's apartment, and I was anxious to see her shoot. Jeff said she was a good shot. Marie and I headed up to say hello to Mr. Johnson and then went to our shooting bay. I was quite inquisitive about all things Marie today. She was classy, feminine, and a real connoisseur of all things lovely. Naturally, I expected her gun to be flashy like mine. Pink, maybe mint green; something that accentuated her beauty. When she opened the big, brown leather purse, she pulled out a plain, black Glock. She loaded the gun, raised her arms to her chest, centered her stance, and let off four rounds: bang, bang, bang, bang. All four shots hit the target, dead center. I wasn't expecting that, but I knew immediately that I had aligned myself with the right person.

Marie and I took turns practicing and I was matching her success, shot for shot. I was feeling quite proud of myself and maybe just a little too confident. I went to load my last few rounds and went to shoot, and it was as if I had lost complete control of my hands. The gun slipped out of my grip and hit the ground. I had already tried to pull the trigger, so it shot straight up causing the bullet to ricochet off the wood frame of the outermost part of the bay. No one was injured, thankfully, but the action brought me right back down to Earth. I was no professional at shooting, and I needed to take this experience and learn from it. I decided it would be best to bring Jeff with me next time and have him work with me. Maybe I wasn't as schooled in this area as I had thought.

Marie made me feel good about the situation. She kept saying that it could happen to anybody, but it didn't happen to just anyone; it happened to me. And why did I lose control of my hands anyway? What caused me to lose my grip? I had been practicing with agile for months. I had hundreds of thoughts racing through my head as Marie continued to gab on the ride back to town. Maybe it wasn't a slip or a fluke. Maybe it was something medical. What if I had something wrong with me? This is unfortunately what it was like living in my head. I just decided to put my negative thoughts away for a bit and try to focus on the rest of our visit.

"Marie, I'm sorry about everything. I still can't understand what happened."

"I told you, Alicia. It was nothing. I'm sure it's happened many times before."

"Maybe...anyway, other than that, I had a nice time with you today. Hopefully, we can do it again sometime soon."

"For sure. I will check in with you tomorrow sometime, but lunch, Friday?"

"Sure. Sounds good."

The cab pulled up in front of my apartment and Marie and I parted ways. It was a good day, overall, but I was praying Jeff was home. I didn't want to be left alone with my racing thoughts. I walked in the door and called out for him, but no response. Apparently, he had got tied up at the newest fixer upper. I pulled out the takeout menus from the drawer next to the refrigerator and skimmed through them. Chinese. That sounds good for tonight. I dialed the restaurant and ordered two number fives and two extra egg rolls. At least I'd have dinner ready for him when he arrived. It had been a long day with a few unexpected twists that stirred up a mix of emotions in me, and all I really wanted to do was eat and then go to bed.

Chinese came about 45 minutes later, and Jeff met the delivery guy at the door.

"Cool, dinner is served," Jeff giggled as he pulled out his wallet to pay. "So, how's my little gun slinger?"

"Oh Jeff, it was just awful! I mean the entire day wasn't, but I had a slip at the range, and it was embarrassing and dangerous." I burst into tears. Something about his presence made me comfortable enough to share all my emotions, but also invited a breakdown, even if unnecessary.

"Baby, I'm sure it wasn't as bad as you're making it seem. What happened, exactly?"

"I went to shoot, and I lost my grip, but not before pulling the trigger. The gun fell from my hands and hit the ground sending the bullet through the wood foundation of the bay. I don't even think anyone saw it but Marie, but it scared the shit out of me, and I was humiliated. I just got a little too confident, I think."

"It sounds like everything turned out okay. That's happened before. I've seen it happen. Let me get you a glass of wine. Eat your food, and we'll go sit in the room and watch one of our old movies. You just need to rest. The past few weeks have been a whirlwind of bullshit and emotions."

I nodded and started eating my chicken and Lo Mein. He was probably right. I'm just tired. He poured us both a glass of wine and we sipped and ate our food. I decided to take a hot shower, if for no other reason than to get the gun residue off from the range, and then I slid into bed with Jeff to watch the film. The night ended peacefully, and I fell to sleep just as the movie began. I remembered the beginning credits and nothing else. When I woke up, I felt better about everything. I decided that I was probably trying to do too much. Jeff was right. So, I planned nothing for today. Absolutely nothing.

As the weekend approached, I wondered what fresh hell was in store for us. Our relationship was such smooth sailing in the beginning, but skeletons from our past kept creeping up, and it was really putting a strain on our plans as well as our relationship. We weren't really talking about it too much, but I could feel the distance slowly moving in, and we were too new to let that happen. I didn't like the feeling. I knew we couldn't avoid conflict forever; it would be nice, but not realistic. When we were alone, things felt perfect, but when we'd let the world in, things became tense. And neither of us were good at conflict, so we'd sleep or drink or have sex to avoid any necessary conversations. And for the most part, that worked for us, but I wasn't so naïve as to think it would work forever.

When Jeff woke up, I asked him if he had anything special he wanted to get into this weekend. It was Friday morning and as usual, we had nothing set in stone for the weekend.

He gave me one of those ornery grins. I smiled and said, "I mean is there anywhere you want or need to go?"

"Not really, Darlin. Maybe a movie if you want to get into that."

"A movie sounds nice. Sunday afternoon? And maybe dinner with Hank and Melinda Saturday night? I'm partial to Marie, but maybe it would be nice to switch it up a little. I was thinking we could stay in tonight though. Just chill for the evening?"

I was a planner and Jeff was not. Aside from his work engagements, he very rarely planned or communicated his intentions. He was good in an immediate situation, like the trip to the Cape, but daily planning was never going to be his thing, and that became a little stressful for me and my organized personality. I was doing my darndest to adapt and to plan and communicate enough for the both of us.

"That works. I'll give Hank a call and see if they're free for Saturday night."

"Sounds good. I'm going to head to the market and grab a few things. Anything you need?"

"Just you darlin."

"Ha, ha. Okay. Be back in a bit."

Jeff was keeping up his appearance with our relationship, but I was already wondering how much of it was genuine. I mean, I know he loves me. In fact, I know he is in love with me, but I often wonder how much a good man can take, even if it's not my fault. I was determined to keep working at us; finding a way to keep the spark even more alive. I grabbed some cheese and crackers, some strawberries and grapes, a cheapy bottle of bubbly, and a can of whip cream. I wholeheartedly planned on making the night worthwhile if we were just "staying in." In addition to stopping at the market, I decided to stop by the local lingerie shop. It wasn't anything exciting, mainly conservative type intimates, but occasionally the owner, Josie, ordered a few borderline risqué items and placed them in the back of the shop.

Normally I would take the ferry to the main shopping mall, but I didn't have time today and I didn't want Jeff to wonder where I was. Josie did not disappoint. She had several new items that she excitedly showed me. She kept them in the back to avoid confrontation with the older, conservative ladies who preferred granny panties and a slingshot for a bra. Josie showed me a plain, lacy red negligée and a black lace one piece with holes cut in places that made me blush. I opted for the red one. I wanted to surprise Jeff, but I didn't want him to have a heart attack. When I went to checkout, Josie said, "I'll give you a great deal on the black one if you want both." I smiled and said, "Sure. Why not? Maybe I'll give it a go closer to the honeymoon." We both giggled and I thanked her and headed back towards our apartment.

"Honey, I'm home. Did you get a hold of Hank?"

"Hey Darlin. Yep, I did. They're free tomorrow night. Wondered if we'd like to take the ferry over to *Big Don's Steakhouse.* I told him yes, tentatively, but I can always call him back and choose a place here."

"Nope. That sounds perfect." It was already late afternoon and I assumed Jeff hadn't had lunch. "Are you hungry? Want to grab an early dinner so we can relax tonight?"

"Sure, let me get cleaned up a bit and we'll head out."

I knew if I phrased it just right I could get him out of the house for a few hours anyway. And he rarely told me no. I just tried to be cautious and let him think that most of the plans were his idea. We hadn't really discussed finances yet and I didn't want him to feel obligated to pay for everything. So, I made it a point to make plans that he seemed genuinely interested in and that, likewise, wouldn't put a huge financial strain on either of us.

Our dinner choices were limited here in Fary Banks for formal dining, and I'd had just about enough of *Anna's Bistro*. I had a few great experiences there, but I've had several horrific confrontations there as well. I was racking my brain to think of where we could go. Takeout was one thing. We had numerous options for that, but actual dining out was a real challenge here. I couldn't help but think to myself that this would be a great opportunity for me or maybe us to open a small, affordable, casual restaurant here in Fary Banks. It would really be beneficial to the community, and it would give us something we could do together. For tonight though, planting a new seed in Jeff's head didn't seem like a great idea, so I decided to just store it away for another day and get to searching online for something that would spark interest for dining tonight.

Places to eat, I thought to myself. Where to go? Nothing specific was jumping out at me. The only places we had regularly frequented were overly formal and quite costly. This made me more uncomfortable than just giving up the dinner date and staying home. So, I moved on to plan B.

"Hey Jeff, what do you think about us running to the seafood market and grabbing some fresh shrimp and lobster and cooking it on the grill here? We could eat on the patio?"

"Sounds good to me. If we're not going out, I don't need to change. I'm ready. Let's go."

And just like that, I took my own opportunity to get out and about and did a 360 convincing him to eat at home. I guess we were still going out together for a bit to collect the food to prepare, but even with my huge desire to socialize publicly, I almost always found a way to retreat.

I grabbed my purse, not that I would need it with Jeff alongside me, but more out of habit. We headed to *Frank's Fresh Seafood Market.* I hadn't frequented the market, primarily because I wasn't that great of a cook, but Jeff was, and I figured it would be a good idea if we started cooking some at home. Maybe he could even teach me a thing or two and next time I could surprise him and prepare our dinner. When we got to the market, Frank had some of the biggest shrimp I'd ever seen. And the lobsters were huge as well. Thankfully, Frank had homemade sauces and seasoned butter for purchase, so it was a one stop shopping experience. After *Franks,* we stopped by the wine shop and grabbed a half a case of red. It was a staple at our house. Maybe too much of a staple at this point. Once we had all the dinner goodies, we headed back home so Jeff could whip up our dinner.

While out by the grill, I ran in the house and freshened up a bit. I put my red negligée on and covered it with a long, button up oxford shirt. I wanted to look sexy, but not so much that I distracted Jeff from the meal preparation. That was for later. Jeff had put a pot on to boil for the lobsters in the kitchen, so I stopped in to check on them. The timer went off just as I approached the pot, so I pulled the lobsters out and placed them on the plate with seasoned butter and carried them out to the patio. Jeff was flipping the shrimp that he had sauteed in garlic butter and then tossed them on a plate. We met at the table and sat down. Jeff had already grabbed a bucket from the kitchen and placed a bottle of red on ice. I opened the bottle and poured us each a glass. Our life seemed perfect, as long as no one else interfered. I relished in the moments that felt like this and tried to regularly remind myself that every moment didn't have to be perfect. I seemed to be regularly allowing my racing thoughts to get in the way of my happiness and this made me question every sigh or look Jeff made. Maybe we were perfectly fine, and it was just me sporadically drumming up bullshit to worry about. That's what it was. I was certain of it. I resigned myself to stop focusing on what could happen and just refocus on what is and was.

Jeff looked up from the table to take a sip and said, "Dear Lord, what are you wearing?" I started giggling just a bit. I wasn't certain if he was pleased or disappointed. There I go again. I stopped and spoke, "I'm wearing one of your dress shirts. Is that okay?"

"Um. Yeah. I'd say it is."

"So, do you not like it? I can change."

"No. I like it. I'd venture to say I like it just about as much as when you're naked. Nothing hotter than a woman wearing your shirt. Especially one of those buttoned up ones. Almost like a present, ready to be opened."

I giggled and blushed a little. "Well, I'm glad you like it. I'm hoping you'll like what's underneath too."

"I already do Darlin. I already do."

Still blushing, "Focus on your lobster Jeff. The night is young."

"Yep Darlin, but we're not," he said laughing.

We enjoyed our dinner and sat on the patio wrapped in each other's arms with the wine that we had left, watching the sun set. The nights were getting shorter and cooler, and it wouldn't be long before we could no longer sit out on the patio without being bundled up. October was sneaking in and soon the cold would too. I wasn't upset about it though. More reason to snuggle up with my love. I was going to work very hard at just being in the moment. Maybe I could find someone to talk to who could help me work through my negative thoughts. I hadn't even tried to find a new therapist since leaving New Jersey. It's probably time. I didn't know much, but I knew I loved Jeff and that I didn't want to be the reason things went astray.

The night went as expected, and Jeff was pleased with my purchase from *Josie's*. Not quite as pleased as he was with his button up shirt, but I should have known that from the start. All was well in our little nest, and I was determined to do everything in my power to keep it that way.

Chapter 25-The Whore Returns

Things were going great considering my hatred for cold icy weather. Fortunately, I had someone warm to return to each day and that made the long, cold, winter days more bearable. That, and a low dose of Prozac.

It was January, and we had not just survived the holidays, we thrived. We had several intimate parties with our close group of friends, and we had not heard a peep from Max or Shelly. I had been going to therapy since the beginning of November and I had found a wonderful therapist to share my fears and concerns with. Dr. Evelyn Jackson was her name, and she was just outside of Fary Banks, making our meetings more discreet, which pleased me. She had suggested several different techniques for me to rely on when I began to have negative thoughts that otherwise felt unwarranted. She helped me to basically get out of my own way to accept happiness.

Dr. Jackson explained to me, in no uncertain terms, that my primary issue was fear of loss because of my relationship with my mother, the loss of my father, and the devastation of being neglected and cheated on by Max. I had never felt worthy of love or happiness and because of this, I had been standing in my own way for most of my life, preventing happiness from finding me. She was a true miracle worker. Jeff and I were growing from her guidance. With only four short months until we planned to say, "I Do," I wanted to make sure that everything was perfect, including my mindset.

I grabbed my purse and headed for the coffee shop. The chill of winter had hit the coast, and the wind stung my face. I had almost made it across the street unscathed by the cold air when a lady I did not recognize attempted to approach me midway through the street.

I looked down and avoided eye contact. The last thing I needed was an awkward interaction considering all the drama that had stirred up last Fall. I wanted to keep my peaceful existence and I honestly just didn't need to be bothered today. I had several things to do before Jeff came home and it was too damn cold to strike up a conversation in the middle of Main Street anyway. She seemed to be pursuing me though, regardless of my less than welcoming demeanor. She was heading directly at me. I could tell from her presentation she had money. Her clothing was designer, and that hair was something artistically created by one of New York's finest stylists, I just knew it. As I glanced up through the scarf tied across my face, I accidentally made eye contact. Dammit. She had bright auburn hair, and she had a familiarity that made my stomach feel a little queasy. Surely to God it couldn't be her? I had only seen one picture of this woman on Jeff's computer, and that was only because I pressed him. I wanted to see a picture of the only other woman that could truly make Jeff's heart skip a beat. Eventually, he gave in and let me see her picture, but only once. Immediately after, he removed it from the gallery and that was that. It was etched in my memory though. You don't forget a face like that, especially when you know how the love of your life felt about her. Still, I wasn't certain it was her.

Between Max and Jeff, I always had the ghost of one of two red-haired beauties haunting me. Until this very moment, I hadn't realized how similar the two looked to one another. It was almost uncanny. Though I just wanted to reach the warmth of the café, I scanned her anyway as she approached.

The woman's shoes alone cost more than my rent; I was sure of it. She was dressed rather inappropriately for the conditions, and a local wouldn't chance wearing those shoes in this weather, let alone spend that kind of money on them. I knew it wasn't coincidence. She crossed my path with a purpose. It was most definitely Jessica. I just knew it.

Keep walking, I kept thinking to myself. As I drew closer, her features became clearer. I had almost completed the path across the street when she locked eyes with me again and said, "Do you by chance have a light? I'm trying to quit these damn things, but the stress you know. And of course, it helps me maintain my figure."

She acted coy, as if I were a stranger, but her body language told a different story.

"Sorry, I do not. I quit when I left New York. Well, officially, New Jersey, but same difference.

Occasionally I use a vape, but no cigarettes." I then thought to myself, Why am I offering up unnecessary information? Why am I even talking to her. Just keep walking.

"New York? Well, that's where I am from, and you do look familiar. I mean we did live in Jersey and then when I returned to the city we moved across the state line to be closer to work."

Chills ran up and down my spine. I felt as if an actual ghost was standing in front of me.

Her voice cracked. It was a distinctive sound; one I had heard before. And it was then that I knew she had me right where she wanted. It wasn't Jessica, Jeff's old flame.

It was her, the whore, I mean Dominque. Dominque Jefferson, the one who swooped in and finished the disaster that was once my marriage to Max. I was confused as to why I connected Jessica and Dominque in my mind. Yes, they both were red-headed beauties, but they honestly didn't look anything alike. And to be fair, I had only seen Jessica's picture once, and I hadn't seen Dominque in over 20 years. I was going to need a trip to Dr. Jackson's today, that's for certain. My mind was beginning to play tricks on me. I felt disoriented. I stood there stunned. I couldn't speak. I felt as if my legs were crumbling beneath me and then I heard the sound of a horn blaring, and down I went. I was struck by something and that's all I remembered.

When I opened my eyes, I noticed familiar surroundings. Here I was, back in the hospital again. I could tell my injuries weren't horribly serious because I could wiggle my toes and the familiarity of the surroundings told me I was at least mildly coherent. The lights were off in the room, but the cracked blind let just enough light in so that I could make-out the faces of Max, the whore, and thankfully, Jeff. What a stone-cold group of weirdos. They didn't know I was conscious yet, so I closed my eyes and tried to listen in. All I could think was what in the Hell was she doing here and furthermore, what the Hell was Max still doing here? And do I tell Jeff that I thought Dominque was Jessica at first? Wonder if he had made the association himself? Boy I had a lot more to uncover in therapy.

Thankfully, Shelly didn't surface, or I would have lost my mind for sure. I heard Jeff tell Max that he needed to leave and that I didn't need any additional stress. I also overheard him ask what she was doing here and even Max acted confused about her presence. It was my understanding that they weren't an item on any level and my interest in Max was null, so why? Just why? Before the conversation could continue, I muttered "Hello."

"She's awake. Thank God," Jeff said as he moved across the room to my bedside.

I leaned forward just a tad to give Jeff a little kiss and it was then that I knew the extent of my injuries. The throbbing just from that little movement of my neck and head told me this wasn't good. "Don't try to move darlin. You're going to be okay, but you'll be sore for a while. The doctor will be in soon. I believe they plan on giving you a neck brace and some good medicine and hopefully surgery won't be necessary. Do you remember what happened?"

"Yes. Max's whore, I mean Dominique, stopped me in the middle of a busy road and asked me for a light. The worst part is that she knew exactly who I was. We had met years ago in the neighborhood bodega in Jersey. We even became acquaintances.

Had several conversations about the necklace he had bought both of us, though she didn't know who I really was. And she was the one that announced her pregnancy to me. I never told Max, but I did tell her. I just skipped town after asking for a divorce. And from what I had understood, she left Max. Apparently, I was wrong. She must have returned once the baby was born. If it was born. Who knows and frankly, who cares? And today, once I realized who she was, it was too late. Boom. A car struck me and now I'm here. Amazingly, she came out unscathed, as usual. Knowing her, she pushed me in front of the car. What kind of idiot strikes up a conversation in the middle of the street anyway?"

Dominique chimed in. "I'm not a whore, but I am sorry that you've been hurt by us, now twice. I'd appreciate it if from now on if you would refer to be by my name."

"I did. I said, "The Whore.""

Dominque sighed loudly. Max stood in front of me, silent for a change. Jeff snickered a little under his breath and I wanted to be mad, but I imagine hearing me refer to Max's fling as "the whore," was a little entertaining.

"Well, you're going to be just fine. I'll walk out and let the nurse know you're awake."

As Jeff left the room, Max headed over towards me. Before he could lean in to do anything I raised my hand and stopped his pursuit.

"Max please do not speak to me. Do not try to explain. Do not touch me. Just take her and get the Hell out of here. I know about her. Knew. I've known since it started and that was the straw that broke the camel's back in our marriage and thank God it did. My understanding was that you two went your separate ways, but regardless, I could care less. Neither of you need anything from me to be happy, so just leave!"

"But Alicia, there is something you need to know." Dominique..."

"Stop right there. I do not care. LEAVE!"

Max shrugged his shoulders and tapped Dominique's arm. "Let's go. We can discuss it with her later."

The two left and I instantly became curious, but not enough to give either of them the satisfaction that I gave a shit about what they thought or had to say. I mean how much more of a shock could they induce besides the adulterous baby and affair? I already knew, and I was way past over it. Plus, I had the love of my life at my side. You don't understand true love until you've experienced a narcissist like Max. You need to understand love and hate to truly feel the difference. The problem was that it took me so long to stop hating Max. If you feel love or hate for someone, you still care. It wasn't until the announcement of the love child that I became indifferent. Indifference is where it's at. Indifference let me leave and start over. I am appreciative of that lesson because it led me to Jeff.

Jeff returned several moments later with the nurse. After several hours of waiting and adjusting medications, they released me. Jeff and I headed back to our apartment. He did not ask any questions and he didn't seem to care. He was just happy that I was safe. He carried me straight to bed. I fell asleep almost instantly in his arms, and once again, I felt safe.

The next morning, I woke up in excruciating pain. My neck was absolutely killing me. I whimpered a little and Jeff must have heard me because he slowly rolled over and touched my face.

"Are you okay darlin? You gave me quite a scare. I'll go get some of your pain medication and make you some coffee. Are you hungry? You really should eat something with the medication."

"I'm not feeling the best. My neck hurts badly, and I have a pounding headache. I'm still a little groggy from all the medication they gave me yesterday. How about some aspirin instead of the narcotics and a piece or two of rye toast? And I'd love a caramel latte from *The Beanery.* You don't have to go and get it. We could order delivery."

As soon as the words came out of my mouth I felt a sense of guilt. This man does everything for me and now I'm suggesting he go out in the blistering cold to get me a latte when we have perfectly good coffee here. I knew he wouldn't fiddle around with delivery for a couple of coffees, and I also knew he'd do anything to make me feel better. I tried to retract my request, but he had already suited up with his toboggan and winter coat.

"I'll run real quick to *The Beanery*, and I'll grab a few sweet treats for later in case you're feeling up to it. Here's a glass of water and some aspirin. I'll make the toast as soon as I get back. Please just stay in bed and rest. And let me know if the aspirin doesn't start to work soon. There's no shame in taking the good stuff for a few days. You were struck hard, and the emotional shit is more than I can handle, so I'm certain you're struggling."

"Thank you sweetheart. I appreciate you more than you'll ever know. See you when you get back."

Jeff left and I laid there lost in my thoughts. I still didn't know what to make of Dominque showing up and clearly I was going to have to deal with her sooner or later. She was here for a purpose, and I feared what the big news might be. I reached gently for the remote and turned on one of our movies. The old black and white films covered me in a sense of peace every time. There was something so serene and tranquil about the lighting, the music, and the innocence of the romantic gestures. We both loved them and honestly, aside from making love, there really wasn't anything we enjoyed doing more together.

About 30 minutes had passed and I started to get a little worried. I knew that it had been spitting snow and the weather forecaster predicted some icy conditions, but Jeff had been wearing his boots and he had been living in this climate for years, so I usually didn't pay the weather any never mind. I tried his cell and of course it began ringing right next to me. He often would leave it behind, and though today it was a bit more annoying because I was worried about him, I loved that he trusted me enough to leave his phone unattended. I rolled over very slowly to avoid hurting my neck any further and I slid my feet to the floor. Luckily, Jeff had placed my slippers at my bedside for me. He knows me well enough to understand that I'm not likely to remain immobile and I guess he wanted me to be prepared. I cautiously slid into the slippers and got to my feet. I began the slow crawl to the kitchen and grabbed a piece of bread from the counter and popped it in the toaster. I waited for it to be finished and held on to the counter for a little extra support. After spreading a little butter on it, I grabbed the slice and nibbled, looking out the front window as the snow hit the sidewalk. Luckily, I had brought my phone with me, so I didn't have to make the trek back to the bedroom. I decided to call *The Beanery* and see if Jeff had at least made it there.

The phone rang three times, and a young girl answered the phone. "Good morning, *The Beanery.*"

"Hello. This is Alicia Lavy. I'm not sure if you know who I am, but..."

The young girl interrupted me.

"Of course, Alicia. I know who you are. I just waited on Jeff. He was interrupted by some red-haired woman while ordering and I could tell he wasn't extremely pleased to be interacting with her, but he quickly managed to get away from her and gather his order. He was pleasant as always and gave me a nice tip. He left about 10 minutes ago. I assume that is why you are calling. He said several times that he needed to hurry to get back to you. Mentioned that you had some minor accident and that he didn't want you to be alone for long."

"Thank you so much. I'm sorry. I didn't get your name."

"Janey. I'm the girl with the short, curly blonde hair. I always forget my name tag, but I am usually the one who waits on the two of you love birds." She giggled.

"Well thanks again, Janey. I really appreciate you letting me know and your great service every time we visit."

"You're most welcome. I hope you are on the mend soon. See you next time you're out and about."

We ended the conversation, and I moved closer to the front window to see if I could see Jeff yet.

Several minutes later, Jeff opened the front door with two lattes in hand and a small paper bag, I assume full of goodies for later. "Darlin, what are you doing out of bed?"

"Well, I got worried about you. You've been gone for a while, and you left your phone here. So, I went in to make a piece of toast and to see if I could see anything from the front window. I called *The Beanery* and spoke to Janey. She said you had an interesting encounter while you were there."

Jeff rolled his eyes and instead of reacting, he just smiled. "Everything is fine. Dominque, is that her name? She approached me and asked if I would arrange for you two to meet in the next few days. Apparently she only plans on being in town until Wednesday. Shit! It's Saturday. I need to call and change our dinner plans for tonight. You need to rest."

"I agree. I think it's best that we stay in for the next few days. So, what did you tell her exactly?"

"I told her to take a pause and that we would reach out when we were ready. If she had to leave, she could just leave. She handed me a business card with her contact information, and I grabbed it and turned my attention back to the order. It took me a while to get there because the sidewalks haven't been salted yet and the wind is gusty and cold. I fear it's going to be a hell of a winter."

Jeff helped me back to my bed and handed me my latte. I had paused the movie so we could watch the rest of it together. He snuggled in beside me the best he could, while having me propped up on several pillows. I had taken the neck brace off. It was just way too uncomfortable. We rested most of the day as well as Sunday and come Monday morning, I was feeling a little less sore and a little more like myself. I asked Jeff for the business card that Dominque had handed him, and I sent her a text asking her to meet us at the deli at noon. I asked Max to attend too. I

wanted this shit to be over.

Chapter 26- Fixing What Wasn't Broken

Jeff had a meeting at the bank already scheduled for 10:00 a.m. prior to my accident and he had no choice but to go. He promised me he would make it to the deli by noon and not to worry. After he left, I slid into my closet to find something I would feel attractive in for this uncomfortable arrangement. Unfortunately, the weather had worsened and whatever I chose to put on needed to be warm enough to sustain the wind and snow. I found an old favorite sweater of mine. I hadn't seen it in years. I had buried it with my memories of New Jersey. In fact, I believe the last time I had worn it I was with Max. I remembered that he loved it, and I knew it would drive him crazy if I chose to wear it today. It was cut low in the chest and lined with a thin layer of lace. Cream in color, it landed right at the top of my waistline. Honestly, I was shocked that a sweater of more than 20 years was still in one piece, let alone fit. I pulled it gently over my neck and looked at myself in the mirror in admiration. Liking myself wasn't an ordinary thing for me and complimenting myself was even less common, but I had to admit, I looked good. I grabbed a pair of skinny jeans from the hanger and because of the weather, heels weren't an option, so I slid on my nice winter boots. After accessorizing a bit, I went into the bathroom and tried to curl my hair, which was quite the struggle with my neck being so bent out of shape. I found a cute cream beanie in my closet and arranged the tendrils of hair around the hat then finished with some texturizing shine spray. I stepped back and gave myself one more check over and I felt hopeful. Hopeful that my hair would remain intact considering the weather. Hopeful my choice of outfit would impress whoever needed impressing. And hopeful whatever had brought these assholes to town would be finished today for good.

I grabbed my gloves, scarf, winter coat and purse on the way out the door and headed towards the deli.

It was windy and the snow had picked up to the point that several inches was covering the ground. Fortunately, our sidewalks had been maintained by the town and therefore weren't as slick as I had been expecting.

I walked cautiously to avoid hurting myself more than I already had. A fall at this point would be catastrophic for me.

The walk didn't take me quite as long as I had expected and before I knew it, I had arrived at the front door of the deli. Even with the cold, I wasn't prepared to walk in without Jeff, so I lingered out front until I saw him approaching. As he walked up he smiled and I suddenly felt warm, almost comforted just by his presence.

"Darlin, you look gorgeous. I love the hat. What do you say we get in here and get this over with?"

I smiled and nodded in agreement. He took my gloved hand and opened the door.

As we entered we noticed the two of them already seated in the back of the restaurant. We approached hesitantly. I could tell we were both thinking of just turning around and saying screw this, but we were both acutely aware that this mess would never be over with if we continued to avoid it.

As we approached the table, Max stood up as if he were pretending to be a gentleman. I dropped eye contact and Jeff noticed my discomfort. Jeff pulled a chair out for me and helped me out of my coat as I slowly and reluctantly took my seat. Jeff sat down quickly beside me and before either of us could say a thing, Max started speaking.

"So, we have some news and we wanted to share it with you two."

As he spoke he stared at me in a way that felt like lasers shooting through me. I knew he recognized the sweater, and I began to regret my choice. Why would I care to make him jealous anyway? I should have dressed more modestly. I already had everything that I could possibly want, and teasing Max should have been the last thing on my mind. I suddenly remembered that I had not reached out to my therapist, and I felt a pressing need to grab my phone and text her for an emergency visit. Instead, I returned my stare back at Max and avoided eye contact with Dominque.

Jeff interrupted. "What the hell is it? I've tried to maintain control here, but I've got to be honest. You two are testing my limits."

"Okay. Well Dominque and I had a child together soon after Alicia left town."

I couldn't remain quiet. "Yes, we know. What does this have to do with me? With us? Jeff, I'm not sitting through this."

Max interjected. "Give me a minute Alicia. I have a point. An important one."

I responded, almost screaming, "Well then get to it."

So, our daughter, Beth, went away to college and was placed with a roommate at random. They became the best of friends. Her roommate, Jennifer, introduced her to a nice gentleman by the name of Jason. Jason Linford.

It was at this point that Jeff jumped to his feet and almost collapsed. I grabbed his arm and pulled him back to the chair, almost throwing myself out of balance.

"Jeff, please. Sit back down and here them out."

"Anyway, I had no idea about Jeff until Shelly reached out. I did some research because, as you know, I had some regrets about losing Alicia. No worries Alicia, I've let that dream go."

Dominque was now looking agitated as she began to speak. "Get on with it, Max."

Max gave her the look that I had experienced so many times in our past and I again felt comforted by how well Jeff loved me.

Max continued. "So, when Beth came home for Christmas she brought her new beau with her. Dominque and I decided years ago that we would spend holidays together for Beth's well-being and we both attended all her milestones together. I guess we felt that it wasn't her fault that we didn't work out, but we desperately wanted her to experience some sense of a family unit. When we were introduced to Jason he explained that his mother, Jessica, had left his father because of his demanding job and the hours that it necessitated. She spoke kindly of him to Beth, but simply said that they just couldn't find common ground. He explained that his dad didn't know about him and that his mother thought that it was for the best. He complimented how Dominque and I had handled our separation regarding raising Beth, and knowing what I knew, I felt like we should reach out and try to connect Jeff with Jason. I'm sorry if this all seems overwhelming, but I wanted to help Beth do this for her now future husband. They surprised us with the news of their engagement at

Christmas as well. So now that you know, Dominque and I will leave you two alone, unless you want to have us help with introductions. I'm confident if you meet Jason, you'll love him. He's such a down to earth, kind-hearted man. I wish that I was more like him. And Beth is wonderful. She's the best part of both of us. She's not quite 20 and has already graduated from her undergraduate program. She's smart and kind, and just a beautiful person. I know this is uncomfortable for you, Alicia, and I am sorry. Nothing like blending two worlds that you want absolutely nothing to do with just months before your wedding, but again, I felt compelled to tell you both; for the two of you and my daughter and future son-in-law."

Shocked didn't even begin to describe my emotions, and hearing Max say that he was sorry was completely unbelievable to me. I tried my best not to roll my eyes and stay focused on how this news was impacting Jeff. I knew, deep down, that Max was enjoying this. Even if he couldn't have me anymore, he could still play a part in my pain, and no matter what he said, I knew this bullshit pleased him.

Jeff just sat there in disbelief. He did not say a single word. I, likewise, just sat there silent. I felt like I should be comforting Jeff in some way, but honestly, it was as much of a shock to me as it was to him, and it most definitely would put a kink in our happily ever after.

The waitress approached the table and asked if we were ready to order. Not one of us could utter a response. She smiled and nodded and said she'd just give us some more time.

Time, I thought. We were going to need some time; I was certain of that.

Chapter 27- Open Arms

Jeff and I sat on the news for the next month. Max and Dominque left soon after our meeting at the deli and I had heard from the gossip brigade that Max had decided not to buy the condo in town. For that I was thankful. Shelly seemed to be a concern of the past and Jeff and I had barely spoken. We lived in the same apartment. We ate meals together and our drinking had increased significantly. We were clearly self-medicating, but we were not communicating. Yes, we made love on occasion, and I wouldn't call it robotic, but it lacked the passion that we had prior to the knowledge of Jeff's son. I had been visiting Dr. Jackson twice a week and none of the strategies she was suggesting seemed to be working. I began to worry that our relationship wouldn't survive this.

The silence was deafening, so I decided enough was enough. It was now the beginning of March, and winter was ending. It was still brisk and chilly outside, but the days were getting longer, and the sun could be felt more dominantly on my skin. The winter blues would soon be a thing of the past and I wanted this dark cloud over our relationship to be in the past as well.

Once awake, I rolled over towards Jeff.

"Hey. Are you awake?"

Almost grunting, he responded with a "Yup."

"Okay Jeff. This ends today. If not, we will. I've had enough. Our wedding is in two short months. Should we even be planning it still or should I call and cancel the arrangements?"

"What? Cancel? Why would you say a stupid thing like that?"

"Stupid? Stupid is the way you have been acting for the past two months. Someone didn't die. Quite the opposite. Someone was born. If you don't want to meet him, fine. If you do, that's also fine. But make a decision. A decision about Jason and a decision about us because I can't live like this anymore. We were so in love and now we're just going through the motions. If this is how it is going to be, then yes, I want to cancel the wedding and move on with my life."

Jeff sat up in the bed. He looked down and I could see tears welling up in his eyes. I had never seen this side of him, and I appreciated that he was able to express his emotions, but it also tore me apart. He collected himself and turned towards me, face to face, for the first time in two months.

"Alicia, I'm sorry. I love you more than anything in this world. I've just been so confused and broken over the deceit. Jessica had no right to keep Jason from me. Of course, I want to meet him and Beth, if you are comfortable with it. And I have no doubt in my mind about spending the rest of my life with you. I'll make this up to you, I promise!"

I leaned in and kissed him, slowly and gently like we used to kiss when we first met. He leaned into me. It felt like it had before and our love making was anything but motionless. When we finished he held me in the nook between his arm and chest; my safe place where I fit perfectly. He whispered, "I'm sorry," again. I simply replied, "I know, honey. I know."

Once we were up and dressed I grabbed the card with Jessica's and Jason's information on it. I stepped out on the patio and made the phone call myself.

The phone rang several times before someone answered. I felt as if I was holding my breath. I became dizzy and for the first time in a long time, I appreciated the cool air on my face. It was probably the only thing keeping me vertical. A deep voice answered the phone with a kind, "Hello."

"Hello. Is this Jason? Jason Linford?"

"Speaking. How can I help you ma'am?"

Ma'am I thought. Polite, but already a kick in the shins. I giggled to myself.

"Hi. My name is Alicia Lavy. My fiancé's name is Jeff Linford. I believe he is your biological dad. I know this is probably awkward, but I assume you have had some time to process this as we met with Beth's parents a few months ago and they mentioned that you had discussed this over the holidays. I wanted to reach out and see if maybe we could arrange a visit sometime soon. That is if you feel up to it. Your father and I will be married on May 28$^{th.}$ and I was rather hoping we could get together before that. If you need some time, I totally understand. I just wanted to get the ball rolling."

"Oh. Okay. Well hello Alicia. It's nice to meet you. I have heard quite a bit about you from Max. Rest assured, all good things. Mom hasn't said much, but to be fair, I don't think she even knew about you until we mentioned your engagement last month. A little awkward, I know, but she seemed pleased about the news. She loved him and always said she just wanted him to be happy. It just wasn't in the cards for them, and she knew that with his schedule, he probably wouldn't have the time to commit to a child. I don't necessarily agree with her choices. I would have loved to have been a part of my father's life growing up, especially since mom never did marry, but I guess it is what it is. So sure. I'd love to meet the two of you. A relationship with Jeff now would be better than never having one at all. We live about three hours from Fary Banks. We just moved into a new place in preparation for my new job, and Beth plans to attend a graduate school close by once she finishes up her master's online. We are getting married in December of this year and we also appreciated that our new home was only several hours from where mom lives as well as Beth's parents, Max and Dominque. Of course, you already know of them. I've heard the story. No need to get into that right now. But yes, central to our families, and now, I guess, not too far from the two of you. Guess we couldn't have planned it any more perfectly in terms of location."

I listened intently and I was so impressed by his kindness and candor.

"Well Jason. Great. When are the two of you free? Maybe we could meet somewhere in between?"

"Honestly, our schedule is open until mid-April. Beth is beginning her master's program in the summer, so she's off until June. I start my new position on April 19th. How about next weekend? We could meet in Chester. It has many accommodations in terms of lodging and restaurants. I could text you a few phone numbers for places to stay if this is your cell. That is if the time frame works with your schedules too."

"Most definitely. We could drive up on Friday evening and meet up on Saturday morning wherever you see fit. Then if things go well, maybe dinner Saturday night?"

"Sounds good to me. I'll text you the details I mentioned. Looking forward to meeting you both in person, Alicia. It was a pleasure talking to you, and thanks so much for reaching out."

"The pleasure is all mine, Jason. I am looking forward to meeting you both as well. Oh, and if it is all the same to you, could you keep this between the four of us for now? My relationship with Max and Dominque, as you know, is a little strained, and I am still working on acceptance and forgiveness. Don't worry, I'll get there. I am certain Beth is a wonderful girl, and this strain will have no bearing on our relationship. I just need a little more time to process this before we all gather as a blended family. And obviously, if you want your mother to be there, I understand, but I'm thinking if all goes well we will stay for the entire weekend. Maybe we could get to know each other first and then she could join us for Sunday brunch? Give you and Jeff a chance to meet first?"

"No problem, Alicia. I totally understand. Meeting my father for the first time will be plenty of an experience without anything extra. And yes, I'm certain mom would enjoy that. She has no animosity over Jeff or the two of you as a couple. I'm sure everything will go smoothly. See you soon."

I hung up the phone and paused to take in a little more air before entering the house to discuss the plans I had prematurely made without disclosing my intentions to Jeff. He did say he wanted to meet Jason. I'm not certain he meant like this, but our relationship truly depended on accepting this and moving forward. I slid my cell in my pocket as I heard the beeps from texts I assumed were from Jason. Slowly I slid open the patio door to approach Jeff and share the news.

"I see you're all dressed and ready for something. Where are you going?"

"Where are we going, you mean? I thought we could spend a little time together. Not just sitting here staring at walls or the television but doing something that we both enjoy. It's probably still a little too chilly to sit on the beach, but I thought maybe a little shopping, lunch, and the range. We haven't had an opportunity to practice together yet and I'd really like to see you shoot."

"Sounds perfect. Let me grab my sweater and gun purse. I have some things to share with you anyway. We'll talk over lunch."

"Okey Dokey, Darlin. I'm ready when you are."

Chapter 28- Moving Forward

Jeff and I walked down Main Street and chose to stop at *The Beanery* for lunch. We hadn't had our morning caffeine fix yet and after all, this was the place where we first fell in love. It seemed nostalgic and necessary at this point. We both ordered paninis and lattes and took a seat at our regular table. As we nibbled and sipped I became increasingly uncomfortable with the conversation that needed to take place, so I decided just to dive in.

"So, Jeff, we didn't have plans this weekend, so I made some. I hope you're okay with that?"

"Sure, Darlin. What are the plans?"

"Okay, now don't get mad. Just hear me out."

Jeff instantly looked irritated. I began to get anxious, but the damage was already done, so I might as well come clean.

"So, when I stepped outside this morning, I took the card that Max had given us and gave Jason a call. He was so very sweet and excited to meet you. He suggested that we meet halfway this weekend. They only live about three hours from all their family now, and I'm sure he will want to share all the details himself, but I agreed to go to Chester this weekend and meet up. We will have Friday night to settle in and then meet them for lunch on Saturday. If all goes well we will have dinner with them too. I asked that Max and Dominque not be told, and we agreed that if you were comfortable with it, Jessica could meet us for brunch Sunday before we head back home. He shared that she never did get married, but was happy, and likewise, was happy for you. I know you're taking this all in and I am so very sorry if you think I have overstepped, but we need some closure if we are getting married in May. And who knows?

Maybe Jason and Beth will want to come and share the day with us."

Jeff just stared blankly at me, silent, and his expression was a little alarming.

"Jeff? Say something, please."

After a deliberate pause, he took a big swig of his latte, sat it down, and leaned in a little. I felt almost frightened until he began to speak.

"Well Alicia, I understand why you arranged all of this, and I'm not mad. I can't say that I'm ready for this yet, though. I'm conflicted. I want a relationship with my son, and I want to meet his fiancé, but honestly, for the first time in my life, I'm scared. I'm angry at Jessica too. There's no earthly excuse to keep my son from me. I should have, at minimum, been given a choice. But fine. We'll go. Let's skip shopping and just go to the range. I think a little shooting therapy would be good for me. And us."

I nodded but didn't say anything else. I finished my sandwich, though I wasn't hungry at all. Quite the opposite. I felt sick and empty, but not hungry.

We finished up at *The Beanery* and found a taxi to take us to *Johnson's Farm*. While riding there I pulled out my phone and clicked on the links Jason had sent me and made a reservation at a nice lodge on the lake in Chester for Friday and Saturday night. Even with the anxiety of the meeting, I did think that Jeff and I spending some time together in a different location would be good for us. As we pulled up to the farm, I received two more texts from Jason with reservations for lunch, dinner, and Sunday brunch. I didn't share any of this information with Jeff. At this point I decided to just let him come along for the ride.

As we entered the farm, Mr. Johnson approached me and gave me an awkward hug. Jeff looked at him and snickered, "I guess she really is a regular here now, huh?"

Mr. Johnson smiled and said, "Alicia is a hoot. We love it when she comes. She brings a little flare to an otherwise dull looking place."

Jeff nodded in agreement and headed towards an open bay. When we entered, I pulled my gun out of the case and loaded it rather quickly. Before Jeff could even get his gun secured, I tossed on my ear protection and fired four shots, hitting dead center of the target.

"Well hells bells, Alicia. I had no idea you were that accurate of a shooter. I better mind my p's and q's from now on when I'm around you."

I giggled and he continued to laugh while he looked at me with an interest I hadn't felt in some time. I could tell this was a big turn on for him, and honestly, that was my hope all along. We took turns shooting and laughing and Mr. Johnson stood behind us watching in amusement. When we finished, we were both so oddly turned on that we could hardly wait to get home. It was exhilarating for some reason, and once we made it back to our apartment, we were undressed before leaving the entryway.

The sex wasn't just good. It was mind blowing. I was positive that this was going to become a regular date plan for the two of us. And we both needed it: The stress relief from shooting and the sex. It was exactly what we needed to move forward. We fell asleep early without dinner, but neither of us minded. We both woke the next morning hungry and oddly content, for the first time in months.

The next few days flew by and suddenly Friday was upon us. I had already packed weekend bags for the two of us and the rental car was scheduled to be delivered any minute. I expected Jeff to be nervous, but he didn't seem to be. He walked out of the bathroom refreshed and handsome as ever.

"Are you ready to go baby? I've got all our stuff sitting by the front door."

"I am. Let's go. I'm ready, I think, to meet my son and start moving forward with our lives. I can't explain it, but I just know deep down things are going to turn around for us and I'm excited about a potential relationship with my son."

I heard a car pull up out front, so I grabbed our bags, smiled at Jeff, and headed out the door.

Chapter 29- Diggin up Bones

The trip wasn't all that long. I expected for the ride to feel excruciating considering the silence surrounding us. We were fine. I knew it, but Jeff was nervous, so I didn't push for conversation. I knew he needed the time to collect his thoughts.

When we pulled up to the lodge I could see a little more life in Jeff's eyes. The place was beautiful. Leaves were slowly starting to form on the trees. Everything seemed to be starting to come back to life, and I was hopeful that Jeff would too.

We entered the large reception area to check in and before we could collect our belongings and our keys, a tall, broad shouldered, handsome man with just a touch of strawberry blonde hair on his chin approached us. He was wearing a hat with Jersey embossed on the front and a Jets sweatshirt. His presence was welcoming and his characteristics oddly familiar. I realized almost instantly that it was Jason. Our plans were to wait until tomorrow for lunch, but here he stood within feet of us, and Jeff seemed to be in a daze. I knew that he knew instantly who he was standing in front of. It was like looking in a mirror if the mirror were 30 years younger. Jeff gently sat his duffel on the floor in front of him and by instinct, walked towards Jason and reached out his arms for a hug. Jason, I assume being raised with good manners, embraced Jeff back without the awkwardness you would expect.

As they exited the embrace, Jeff began to speak.

"Hi Jason. I am Jeff, as you probably already know. I'm your father. I'm so excited to finally meet you."

"I feel the same Jeff, or Dad, if it's okay that I call you that. I know this is awkward, but I'd like to skip all the formalities and just take this moment at face value. You didn't know about me. You didn't abandon me or neglect me. Our lack of relationship all these years is no fault of your own. So, I suggest we just pick up here and start building something worth remembering. That is if you feel the same way. And I know this will be difficult because I have asked mom to join us tomorrow but try not to feel animosity for her. She was young and did what she thought was best. It's best left in the past. I'm happy. She's happy. You and Alicia are happy. Let's just be happy."

Jeff paused for a minute, but he was smiling from ear to ear, so I felt comfortable with what was coming next.

"Most definitely. I am so impressed with how mature you are about all of this. It seems you are a bit more settled, emotionally, than I was when I found out. And for that, I am so very proud. Jessica has clearly done a wonderful job of raising you. She was always a wonderful person, and I'm sure she still is. How would you feel about an early dinner tonight as well?"

"Sounds perfect. Let me take the rest of our things up to our room and change. I'll grab Beth and we can meet you at the restaurant here at the lodge. Say in an hour if that works?"

"Great. We will do the same and freshen up and see you soon. I am excited to meet Beth and so glad that I get a chance to know you."

They shook hands, which seemed odd after the big embrace, but I think the masculinity took control once they had officially met.

As Jason turned and walked away, Jeff turned around and placed a big kiss on my lips.

"As usual, you were right. Thank you for arranging

this. I am happy we are here, and even happier that I am doing this with you. I love you, Alicia."

I smiled and nodded in agreement. "I love you, too."

Once we made it to the room, we tossed our belongings in the closet and freshened up a bit. I ordered a bottle of red from the front desk and the bellhop delivered it with 20 minutes to spare. I poured us both a glass and toasted Jeff to new beginnings. We drank the wine and then headed down to the lodge to meet Beth and to continue getting to know Jason.

As we entered the restaurant I was taken aback by all the trophies mounted on the wall. Afterall, we were at a lodge by the lake, but boy were there a bunch of them. I had never been fond of hunting unless out of necessity, and these displays seemed extreme, so I tried to refocus my attention on the task at hand.

In a corner booth I noticed Jason waving to us. As we headed to our seats I caught a glimpse of a beautiful young woman. She was only partially standing in an effort to welcome us over, but I could tell she was tall and slender. She had several freckles that peppered her cheeks and the most beautiful long auburn colored hair. Her eyes were a piercing green, not unlike Jeff, and her pretty, white teeth were visible as she smiled. She looked a lot like Dominque, but her stature and confidence screamed, Max. I tried to avoid any negative connotation and just focused on the beauty that was directly in front of me. This was no time for me to feel sorry for myself, and why would I? The true love of my life was holding my hand, rather firmly I might add, and guiding me to the table.

As we approached, Beth reached her hand out to greet us.

"Hello Alicia and Jeff. I'm Beth. So glad to finally meet both of you. I've heard lots about you from mom and dad and I'm so excited for you two to get to know the two of us. The more the merrier, I always say." She smiled again, coyly, and took her seat.

"So, we meet again...Dad and Alicia. Sorry. It sounds so weird when I say that. It's going to take a little getting used to, but don't' worry, I like the way it sounds."

The meal went smoothly, and the conversation was pleasant and flowing. We sat for several hours just sipping wine and nibbling on what was left of our meals. We decided to share a dessert platter, which I might add was delicious, and I even grew to appreciate the wall décor and eccentric music playing in the lodge. I think it was more of the company than the atmosphere, but I felt a sense of peace. When the evening was over we discussed the plans for tomorrow and Sunday and then called it a night.

Jeff and I slept hard and when we woke we felt refreshed and honestly, ready for just about anything. The day went as planned and each meeting seemed more and more comfortable. By the end of our dinner on Saturday night it felt as if we had known Beth and Jason all our life. The stigma of the lost years seemed to vanish, and I had never seen Jeff happier. As we bid adieu for the second evening together, Jeff and I decided to take a walk around the property to see what we could get in to. We hadn't had very much alone time since we arrived.

The paths around the property were well lit and it was truly a breathtaking view; trees for as far as the eye could see and beautiful foliage starting to bud. We walked down by the lake and took a seat on the bank. We just held hands and looked out as the moonlight began to fall on the water. We didn't really say much. We just took it all in. And again, once we hit the bed, we were out. It was a peaceful sleep and we both needed this rest to revive ourselves and our relationships.

Sunday brunch rolled around, and I knew that this might be the most awkward encounter yet. I was about to meet the woman that my Jeff loved first and foremost. The one who broke his heart and the one who only my heart was able to heal. And even though Jeff claimed he held no animosity over the secret of his son's existence, I knew better, and I became increasingly concerned as the time to meet drew closer. Aside from his discontent for her abandonment, I was a little worried that he might see her again and decide he wanted her back. And where would that leave me? I knew deep down that seemed silly, but my heart just couldn't take being left again, especially while sitting across from the love child of my first heartbreak. I suddenly felt a new appreciation for myself. How mature it was that I had accepted all of this, even welcomed it, for the betterment of Jeff. It was without any real concern for my feelings, and I'm certain he hadn't taken the time to even think about it, but I was proud of myself.

"Let's go Jeff. We need to leave now if we are going to make it to brunch on time. Double check the room, would you? I want to make sure we have everything since we plan to head back afterwards."

"I already checked Darlin. I've got everything and I'm taking it to the car now. I'll check out for us and pick you up at the front door. Sound good?"

I smiled and nodded, and he left with our things. I stood in front of the bathroom mirror and stared at myself for a few minutes.

"You are strong. You are beautiful. You are deserving of good things and if you believe it, good things will continue to happen for you."

These were catch phrases that my therapist had encouraged me to say to myself. She wanted me to see them. Say them. Do them. Believe them. And the theory was that I would begin to embody the characteristics genuinely once they became an intricate part of me. I was starting to think this was a whole bunch of bullshit, but I said them anyway. I popped a Prozac and a Xanax for safe measure and chased them with the last swig of wine from the bottle next to the bed, and off I went.

We arrived at Chateau de' Sprig with 10 minutes to spare. I couldn't help but think to myself, what kind of crap do they serve at a place called de' Sprig? Twigs? Grass clippings? I could feel myself getting negative and I didn't want Jeff to sense my frustration, so I plastered a smile on my face and did my darndest to block it out.

We walked in and I headed straight for the bar. I didn't even wait on Jeff, which he probably thought to be odd.

"One shot of vodka, a slice of lemon, and a glass of your finest sweet red wine, please. Never mind, make that a bottle. Thanks."

As Jeff approached, I hurried and downed the shot of vodka and sucked the lemon and tossed it aside. Then I grabbed the two glasses of wine and the rest of the bottle and handed him a glass.

"Thought we could use a drink, huh?" He nodded and I was hopeful that he didn't see me shoot the vodka just before he walked up.

We looked around for Jason and Beth, but they weren't anywhere in plain sight. I turned back towards the bar tender and winked and said, "I'll take a shot of vodka for the two of us." He knew not to mention my first shot by my expression and tone. Without hesitation, Jeff grabbed the shot, clinked it to mine and down they went. As Jeff went to turn around to scan the restaurant once more, he was greeted face to face with a stunning red head. There she stood, average height, large breasts which were fully exposed in her low-cut blouse, and jeans I'm certain she couldn't breathe in. She was gorgeous. She looked uncomfortable, but gorgeous.

"Well, howdy stranger. It's been a long time. You look well."

Jeff smiled and leaned in to give her a half hug. I could tell he was being careful with his reaction and in his mannerisms.

"It certainly has Dar..." And Jeff cut himself off. "Jessica. Nice to see you."

He was about to call her "Darlin." I knew it was out of habit, a term of endearment that he used, but it just about sent me through the roof. He should have just said it. The intent was already there. The damage was done. But I held it together. Today wasn't about me and we could discuss my feelings on the way home.

He sounded so uncomfortable, especially after almost referring to her as he does me, and the same part of me that loves him with my whole heart felt sad for him. It was apparent he had feelings for her as well, and I tried to empathize instead of feeling broken. My heart was officially at war with itself. So, I decided to get away from the situation for a bit.

"Excuse me. We haven't formally met, and my fiancé here doesn't always have the best of manners in stressful situations, but I'm sure you already knew that. I'm Alicia. And I'll be right back."

Before either of them could respond, I turned and headed for the lady's room. Once there, I ran into a stall, locked the door and began to cry. I had to let it out. I had been so calm and so supportive through all of this, but I was at my breaking point. I was fully aware that I was overreacting, and that Jeff did not call her that with intent. I had no doubt about how he felt about me, but I wasn't positive that his feelings for Jessica had completely vanished. And I understood that. Still, this was a lot, and mixing these emotions with medication, two shots of vodka, a glass of wine and an empty stomach was probably not the best choice. I had almost got myself under control when I heard a voice outside of my stall.

"Alicia. It's Jessica. I know this is awkward and you don't know me, but honey come out and let's talk. Just us girls."

She seemed nice and genuine, and I honestly, deep down, felt sorry for her. She got the busy, younger version of Jeff who had a demanding schedule and a crazy loon for an ex. I got the best of him; the retired, open-minded, free-spirited version of Jeff, and one that didn't give two shits about his ex and her antics, and I was sure this was hard for her to digest. And I knew it was important for them to rebuild some sort of relationship for their son and his new wife to be. And I didn't even want to think about what holidays might look like if they had children. Would we all gather as one big happy family with Max and Dominque staring at us around the table? It was just too much to process.

I opened the stall door and Jessica handed me a tissue.

"Now, now honey. There's nothing to be upset about. Jeff and I are more like old friends. Honestly,

I don't even know what to say to him. I mean I hid the fact that he had a child for all these years, so he should be furious with me. It's not his nature though, as you are fully aware. I just want us all to find peace in the situation, maybe even become friends, and be comfortable together when it's necessary for the kids. And I know all about your situation with Dominque, and honey, I'm so sorry. Honestly, because of that alone, I'll never like that bitch."

Finally, I laughed. Then we both started laughing almost uncontrollably. It seemed natural. Tears and laughter were the common reaction to pain, and I was thankful that we could laugh like this. We both apparently needed the release.

"Thank you, Jessica. I'm sorry for my behavior. I might have mixed my medicine with a little too much to drink. Alcohol is never a good thing when you're already emotional, much less with a little dose of Xanax."

"I got you honey, and I totally understand. I can already tell that I am going to like you. Who knows, we might become great friends, and that would be worth it to drive old Jeff a little crazy."

We both started laughing again and then she pulled some makeup out of her purse and helped me freshen up a bit.

"Thanks again. I appreciate you being so kind and understanding."

"Don't mention it doll. Now let's go get this awkward shit over with, what do you think? Maybe get a little food in your stomach?"

"Sounds good to me."

And we exited the lady's room together. As we approached where we had left Jeff standing we noticed that he had moved towards the back of the bar area. Beth, Jason, and Jeff had went ahead and found a table for us to join. We both smiled and took our seats. I could tell Jeff was incredibly nervous. Not about the brunch, or his son, or even Jessica. Worried about whatever it was that Jessica and I had been discussing in the lady's room. The server stopped at the table to take a drink order. Everyone ordered a mimosa or cocktail. I chose to stick with water. That's when I could tell Jeff became worried.

The meal was quaint, and the conversation seemed to flow. As minutes turned into hours, I became increasingly more comfortable in our company. Jeff and Jessica seemed to be getting along in an appropriate manner, and Jason acted as if he had known Jeff his entire life. I chalked that up once again to wonderful parenting on Jessica's part, though I still thought it to be wrong that she had withheld so much from Jeff. By hour two I felt ready to order a glass of red, and it seemed to put Jeff's mind at ease to know that I had become comfortable enough to have another glass. The afternoon ended with goodbyes and plans to meet up again soon, and Jeff and I began the trip back to Fary Banks.

Once in the car, I could tell he wasn't certain what to say to me, so I started the dialogue.

"Jeff, I'm not mad about anything. No need to harp on any of it. I was uncomfortable, a little tipsy, and you unintentionally hurt my feelings. That's it. Everything turned out fine and I'm happy for you. I like Jessica and I love Beth and Jason. Everything will be fine."

Instead of responding, Jeff just nodded and let out a sigh of relief. He turned on the radio to some slow jazz, which always seemed to calm us, and we just

existed peacefully for the rest of the trip home.

Chapter 30- Final Preparations

March and April came and went, and everything seemed to be back to normal. Jeff was talking to Jason regularly and their relationship seemed to be building. Jessica had even reached out to me a few times, primarily just texting me silly memes and a few videos, but I was feeling comfortable with our new friendship, and I was hopeful things would continue to go smoothly. It was what was best for everyone, and I wanted a peaceful existence for all of us.

It was already the second week of May, and our wedding was only a few short weeks away. I had checked in with the caterers and the bakery and verified all the flower arrangements and bouquets. I had one last fitting for my dress this week and other than that, everything was ready to go. We had decided to invite Beth and Jason as well as Jessica but decided against asking Max and Dominque.

Honestly, no good could come of their attendance and this was supposed to be the biggest day of our lives. Neither of us wanted to take the chance that someone or something could ruin it for us. Melinda and Marie agreed to stand up beside me as bridesmaids and we were going to have a little bachelorette shindig this weekend. They invited Beth and Jessica and I agreed, the more the merrier. They really had turned out to be good friends and I was thankful to have met them. Hank and Joe were having a bachelor party for Jeff at the pub and Jeff decided to ask Jason if he wanted to be his best man. It was so sweet the way Jason responded with such enthusiasm. With only a few short months of getting to know each other, I loved how quickly they were building a bond as father and son. Everything seemed to be falling into place.

The days came and went, and the fitting and parties went on without a hitch. The rehearsal dinner was upon us. Only one day until I became Mrs. Jeff Linford. I was so very excited! Our small group of friends and family gathered at *Anna's Bar and Bistro* for dinner, the location of our first date. He arranged for the meal to be the same as we had the first time: French bread, spring mix with house vinaigrette, filet mignon, lobster, whipped potatoes, and seasonal vegetables. It was so delicious, and I ate every bite. Everyone did. I began to worry just a little if my dress would even fit me tomorrow afternoon after such a large meal.

The conversation flowed and Hank and Marie both gave a toast. It was quite lovely. All of it.

Once we were finished with the dinner and the rehearsal itself, I went back to my apartment with Beth and the other girls. Jeff stayed at Hanks. We decided that maybe we should follow the night before the wedding traditions, just in case. The idea seemed a little outdated, but I thought it was sweet that Jeff believed in tradition, so I went along with it.

The girls and I watched movies and drank wine. We had a wonderful time together. I had finally come full circle with my dreams. I had a home full of friends to enjoy, a storybook kind of love, and a life that I didn't need a vacation from. Everything was as close to perfect as it could get.

When morning came, the girls helped me gather my gown and accessories and we were off to the salon. Fortunately for me, the salon was located on the boardwalk close to the beachfront setup we had for our wedding, so Lana, the owner, agreed to let us get dressed in her backroom after she was finished with our hair and makeup. While curling my hair and securing pieces up, styled intricately around my veil,

I watched through the front window as the florist hustled to put the finishing touches on the aisles. A tent was set up with folding tables, decorated with delicate, lace tablecloths and the caterer had already started setting up the buffet. We originally wanted to have the smallish reception on our patio, but with the last-minute influx of guests, we were afraid our little home couldn't accommodate it.

Here I was, mere minutes from walking down the aisle, and I felt no anxiety, no regret. I was certain I was making the right decision, and I could hardly wait.

The girls helped me into my dress to avoid messing up Lana's creations, and then we headed out to prepare to line up for the ceremony. Originally only planning on a small ceremony with three rows for guests, our wedding celebration had grown just a tad. I was happy that we had flourished in our friendships and had made our small circle a little larger. It was comforting to see so many people here to join in the celebration of our big day.

Jeff and I had no reason to be worried about any surprise visitors, but after the year that we had and just preventatively, I had Marie bring my gun purse and place it to the left of the altar. I knew it seemed silly, but I wasn't taking any chances today.

Marie found her place back in the line and the organ began to play "Here Comes the Bride." After the ladies walked down the aisle and took their places, the final march commenced and I began my last walk alone, my last few moments as an unmarried woman. I could see my handsome groom at the altar, smiling at me and giving me that look that he gives with those piercing green eyes. Old green eyes. I loved him so. As I walked, I thought about everything that I had been through and how much I wish my daddy could have been here to give me away. To avoid tears, I took my eyes off Jeff and focused on the bouquet in my hand, careful not to trip on my heels. The white rose in the center was what it was about. Friendship. Friendship led to love. The red roses wouldn't have existed without the foundation of the white one in the center, and neither would our relationship. Maybe that should be my vow to Jeff. To be his white rose first and his red rose second. He would understand exactly what I meant, and it was a perfect metaphor for our love story.

As I neared the end of the aisle, I reached the altar and handed off my bouquet to Marie. Jeff reached for my hands, and I turned to face him.

"The minister began, "Dearly Beloved, we are gathered here today..." and he cutout.

His microphone suddenly stopped working and then a loud pounding sound followed by a loud thud. Something huge had fallen or blown up close to the boardwalk. We turned our stance away from one another and towards our guests where the odd sounds were apparently coming from. When we turned back to face each other, a figure wearing a black dress and veil stood where the minister had been moments before. I had no clue what was going on, but I signaled to Marie to grab my gun.

Frightened, she did as I said. The woman started carrying on about commitment and lying and how marriage was an outdated concept and that neither of us nor anyone else for that matter should ever get married. She somehow had retrieved the minister's pocket microphone, and her chaos was being broadcasted across the boardwalk. The black veil she was wearing covered her face and neither of us could make out who she was. I stepped back several steps and Jeff followed suit. Normally he would have jumped in to protect me, but the shock of the scene had him dumbfounded. Marie gently slid my gun into my left hand, Jeff still holding my right. I slid my right hand out of Jeff's grip and stepped back to the middle of the aisle.

Jeff called out, "Alicia, where are you going? Please come back up here with me. Can we get security? Anyone. Call 911 somebody. This looney is ruining our wedding."

Jeff moved a few steps closer to the crazy woman to subdue her, but as he approached she pulled a pistol out from under the folds of her dress. Jeff instinctively put his hands up and yelled at her.

"Listen, we don't want any trouble. Clearly you need help. Let me get you some. Everyone else, stay in your seats and stay calm. How are we doing with security?"

The veiled lady raised her left hand and flipped the veil off exposing her face.

Oh my God! It was Shelly.

Jeff looked at her with a little sadness and I could tell he thought he could reason with her. My gun was still behind my back, hiding under the bow attached to the back of my waistline.

Jeff attempted to reason with her anyway.

"Shelly. What is this all about? Calm down and lower the pistol. I'll get you the help you need. I promise, but you need to leave for today. Let us have our wedding. SECURITY?"

Shelly held the gun with conviction and lunged back. She looked confident and prepared; odd considering she was wearing that huge, hideous-looking black dress. I became more and more angered.

Her hand grip was high, and she had her index finger already on the trigger. I couldn't wait any longer, and I knew that after all of this, ruining my wedding day, she'd never leave us in peace. If that meant I'd spend a little time in jail for defending my friends and family, so be it.

At this point she had complete control, and I was planning on taking it away from her, now!

"Jeff, step back."

"Alicia, just stay back there and let me handle this."

"Jeff, I'm serious step off to the side and back. Now, please."

Shelly moved two steps forward, not affecting her stance whatsoever. In any other scenario, I would have been impressed with her poise and dexterity, but this crazy Bitch was here to destroy my wedding.

To destroy my life. And I had no plans of letting her!

"Shelly, I'm asking once, nicely, for you to leave.

Turn around. Walk away. Pretend this never

happened."

Jeff was shaking his head, and I was mortified that

he'd hop in front of the gun to protect me.

Shelly refused.

"No Alicia. I'm not going anywhere. And neither are

you. If I can't have my happily ever after, you can't

have yours either."

I then pulled my gun from behind my back and

pointed it at Shelly.

"Leave, or I'll make you leave."

Jeff dismayed by the view, began screaming at me in

a tone that sounded angered and desperate. "Alicia,

what are you doing? Put that damn gun down! She's not worth it! Why do you even have your gun here? AT OUR WEDDING!"

I looked at him with a tear streaking down my face. I didn't have time to explain.

"Jeff, I know what I'm doing. Just step back and trust me, please."

At this point, Shelly became agitated. It was evident in her glare. I could tell she was taking it all in and was becoming increasingly more angered. She then readjusted her aim towards me, and I knew in that instant that she was going to shoot, so I screamed, "Everybody get down," and I aimed for her leg and fired. I just wanted to disable her, not kill her, so we could get her the help that she so desperately needed.

As the bullet soared through the air, still aimed for Shelly's right leg, she let off a shot and I ducked. Jeff must have known she'd retaliate, and he jumped in front of her to stop the shot. My bullet, the one intended for Shelly, struck Jeff on the left side of his back, and he went down, hard. Shelly ran off before the police arrived at the scene. I ran to Jeff and kneeled beside him.

"Jeff, hold on. The ambulance is coming."

"Did they get Shelly? Where's Shelly?"

"She ran off. Don't worry about her. Oh my God, is somebody going to help me?"

Jeff's breathing was getting shallow. Jason ripped off his vest and put as much pressure as possible on the wound on Jeff's back. My white wedding dress was covered in blood. I had blood on my face and my veil. It was everywhere.

The love of my life was literally drowning in his own blood. I sat there and sobbed, wishing there was more I could do. The paramedics finally arrived and patched what they could on the scene, hooked up an IV, and took Jeff off to the hospital.

I sat there on the sand for a few minutes and just wept. Jessica came over to me and kneeled beside me. "Jason rode in the ambulance with his dad."

I nodded as tears dripped from my eyes and saturated my face. With mascara running across my cheeks, and eyes unable to focus, I attempted to look up at her.

"It doesn't look good, Jessica. It doesn't look good."

"I know honey. Let's get you cleaned up and get to the hospital."

End of Book 1: To Be Continued

Look for Book #2 in this series:
Available in November of 2024:

From This Moment On

Acknowledgement

A special acknowledgement to two very different men that I have loved. Luckily, they are the same person.

About the Author

H.E. Burford, is a retired High School English teacher and writing professor, currently living in the small coastal town of Mathews, Virginia. She is originally from Zanesville, Ohio and spent much of her life in Fort Wayne, Indiana. She has been married to her husband, Chris, for almost 27 years and has three grown children, Chloe, Kristian, and Caleb. Aside from writing, Heather enjoys spending time with her beagles and cats and being outdoors. She holds an Associate's of Arts degree, a Bachelor of Arts degree in English with a focus in writing and poetry, a Master of Teaching Degree in Teaching English Education, and a Doctorate in Teacher Leadership, ABD. *In the Moment* is her first published novel. It is the first of a series of three novels, dubbed, *The Moment Series*, focused on the fictional town of Fary Banks, Maine.